# Destiny

## CeeCee Crow

Copyright © 2026 CeeCee Crow

All rights reserved.

No part of this publication may be copied, reproduced, distributed, or transmitted in any form or by any means—electronic, mechanical, photocopying, recording, or otherwise—without the prior written permission of the publisher, except in the case of brief quotations used in reviews or other noncommercial purposes permitted by copyright law.

This is a work of fiction. Names, characters, places, and events are either products of the author's imagination or used fictitiously. Any resemblance to actual persons, living or dead, or actual events is purely coincidental.

Print ISBN:   978-1-971405-11-7

Publisher: Smut by Design

CeeCeeCrow.com

*No matter how dark it gets, never let anyone or anything extinguish the fire inside you.*

# Content Warnings

Thank you for reading Destiny! This book contains themes and content that may be triggering to some readers. Please review the following warnings before proceeding:

## Major Content Warnings:

### Trauma & Neglect

- Childhood trauma & parental death
- Homelessness & survival on the streets
- Starvation & food insecurity
- Scars from past neglect

## Emotional & Psychological Themes

- Hypervigilance & trust issues
- Self-worth struggles & feeling like an outsider
- Panic attacks & dissociation
- Touch aversion

## Harassment & Power Dynamics

- Bullying & verbal harassment
- Unwanted physical contact
- Threats & intimidation
- Systemic oppression & forced containment
- Interrogation by authority figures

## Physical & Supernatural Elements

- Uncontrolled supernatural abilities
- Physical pain from transformation
- Medical examination
- Loss of autonomy

## Romance & Intimacy

- Reverse harem romance (one woman, multiple male love interests)

- Explicit sexual content

- First-time intimacy on-page

- Possessive/protective male characters

- Fated mates trope

## Additional Notes

- Strong language throughout

- References to violence & fighting

- Cliffhanger ending

This list is provided to ensure a safe reading experience. If any of these topics are personally distressing, please read with care.

Thank you for your support and for stepping into Nova's journey.

## Contents

1. Nova — 1
2. Nova — 9
3. Locke — 17
4. Nova — 25
5. Kyron — 33
6. Nova — 39
7. Beckett — 45
8. Nova — 53
9. Nova — 59
10. Nova — 67
11. Vaelor — 71
12. Nova — 77
13. Nova — 83
14. Trey — 87
15. Rane — 91
16. Nova — 97

| | | |
|---|---|---|
| 17. | Locke | 107 |
| 18. | Nova | 115 |
| 19. | Beckett | 121 |
| 20. | Nova | 125 |
| 21. | Trey | 129 |
| 22. | Vaelor | 133 |
| 23. | Nova | 141 |
| 24. | Kyron | 149 |
| 25. | Trey | 155 |
| 26. | Nova | 163 |
| 27. | Nova | 175 |
| 28. | Locke | 181 |
| 29. | Nova | 185 |
| 30. | Nova | 189 |
| 31. | Nova | 197 |
| 32. | Rane | 203 |
| 33. | Nova | 213 |
| 34. | Beckett | 219 |
| 35. | Vaelor | 225 |
| 36. | Nova | 231 |
| 37. | Nova | 239 |
| 38. | Kyron | 245 |

| 39. Nova | 257 |
| 40. Kyron | 263 |
| 41. Nova | 273 |
| 42. Kyron | 279 |
| Thank You | 283 |
| About The Author | 285 |
| Other Books By CeeCee Crow | 287 |

# Chapter 1
## Nova

I wake up cold, which means I woke up.

The alley is one I've used before—two walls cutting the wind, an overhang that keeps the rain off if I press close enough to the stone, and a sightline to the street that lets me hear footsteps before they arrive. I found it three weeks ago and I've been rationing it since, never two nights in a row, never enough to become predictable.

My body does its inventory without permission. Stiff neck. Empty stomach. The cold that stopped being cold somewhere around year three and just became weather. There's pain in my hip from the cobblestones but I don't look at it. Looking at things makes them real.

I sit up slow, keeping my shoulders against the wall, and listen.

The territory is waking up. Carts. Shutters. Someone shouting about prior-day bread, which means the bakery on Venn Street is already setting out and if I move now I can be there before the crowd thickens. I'm calculating the route when I hear footsteps that don't belong.

Too even, too patient—not drunk, not lost, not in a hurry to be somewhere else.

I'm on my feet before they round the corner, which is the only reason I'm standing when they see me instead of sitting. Small advantage. Probably doesn't matter. But I've stayed alive this long by collecting small advantages.

Two men. Not territory watch—the uniforms are wrong, darker and better fitted, with an insignia I don't recognize. They stop at the mouth of the alley like they expected to find me here.

Maybe they did.

"Miss," the taller one says, polite and bored, like this is the third stop on a long shift. "We need you to come with us."

"I think you have me confused with someone."

"We don't."

His partner shifts his weight slightly. Not blocking the alley exit, but filling the space in a way that makes it clear the exit isn't really an option.

I know how to read people. Fifteen years of practice. Loud ones are scared—they escalate because they're not sure they can back it up. Calm ones already know how this ends.

These two are calm.

"What's this about?"

"Just routine verification."

"I haven't done anything."

"Then it won't take long."

I could run. There's a gap between the building to my left and the wall behind me, barely wide enough for my shoulders. I've used it before. If I'm fast, if they're slower than they look, if I can get to the next street before they figure out where I went—

But running means being chased. Being chased means being seen. Being seen means someone remembers my face, and the whole point of the last fifteen years has been making sure no one remembers my face.

I've survived this long by being forgettable.

"Fine."

The street is bright and ordinary and completely wrong.

I've walked this route a hundred times, but always early morning or late night, always slipping between the crowds instead of through them. Now it's full daylight and I'm flanked by uniforms and I'm aware of myself in a way I haven't been in years—the smell of the alley still on my clothes, the way people's eyes slide past me, the space the officers take up on either side.

Two people escorting a woman who isn't struggling. Nothing interesting. Nothing worth a second look.

That's what I'd think if I saw me.

Four blocks. Five. They guide me toward a building I've walked past a hundred times without seeing it. Gray stone, narrow windows, a door like every other administrative door in the district. The kind of place that processes people into paper and files the paper away.

Inside is clean and quiet and somehow worse than the alley. A waiting area with a desk and a few chairs and a hallway that leads somewhere I can't see. The whole place smells like nothing—like someone scrubbed out anything human and left antiseptic behind.

"Have a seat."

One officer disappears down the hallway. The other stays by the door, watching me while pretending not to.

I sit while counting exits, trying not to be obvious. Front door behind me, occupied. Hallway ahead, unknown. No windows. The chair I'm sitting in is bolted to the floor.

This is fine. Vagrancy check, probably. Maybe a relocation sweep. I've been through this before—not here, not this building, but the same kind of processing. Answer the questions, don't volunteer anything, be boring enough that they stamp a form and send you on your way.

I'm good at being boring.

Five minutes pass. Ten. Fifteen.

The officer by the door hasn't moved.

I'm starting to wonder about the bread on Venn Street—whether it's gone by now, whether I'll have to find something else, whether any of this is going to matter by the time they let me out of here—when a door opens at the end of the hallway.

A woman emerges—middle-aged, plain professional clothes, carrying a folder. She doesn't look at me.

"This way."

I follow her to a smaller room with a table that's seen better days, two chairs, no windows. She sits on one side and opens the folder and uncaps a pen like she's done this ten thousand times before.

I take the other chair.

"Name?"

"Nova."

"Age?"

"Twenty-six."

"Place of residence?"

"Between places."

"House affiliation?"

"Dream." The lie is automatic. "Originally."

She writes it all down without looking up. I've done this before. Different buildings, different officers, same bored questions. You give them what they want, nothing extra, and they lose interest and let you go.

"Show me your mark."

My stomach tightens.

"Wrist," she says.

And just like that, I'm awake.

I've been here before too—this exact moment, different rooms. This is where I smile and deflect and show them something fast enough that they don't look too close. A flash of skin, a muttered excuse about fading or placement or a birthmark that confuses people. It's worked before. It's always worked before.

But she's not even looking at me. She's looking at the folder, pen ready, waiting for me to comply so she can move to the next box.

"I'm in a hurry," I try.

"Wrist."

I push up my sleeve.

The skin is pale. Bare. The same as it's been every day of my life.

She glances at it. "Other one."

I show her.

Nothing.

She makes a note. No reaction. No surprise. Just pen moving on paper.

The silence that follows is the first wrong thing.

"It's a late bloom," I say. "It happens—"

"When did you last present for intake?"

The word lands like ice water.

*Intake.*

I'm ten years old. Crouched behind a door I'm not supposed to be near, listening to adults use words I don't understand. *Noncompliant. Unregistered. Containment.* I didn't know what they meant then.

I know now.

"I asked you a question."

"Never."

It comes out too quiet. She writes it down anyway.

"That's not possible," she says, still writing. "Intake is mandatory. There are systems."

"And yet."

She stands. Goes to the door. Speaks to someone I can't see—low murmur, words I can't make out. When she comes back, she doesn't sit.

"You'll remain here."

"For how long?"

"Until verification is complete."

"What does that—"

"A physician will confirm there's no mark present. After that, we'll determine next steps."

"And if I want to leave?"

She picks up the folder.

"Someone will escort you to a holding room. You'll have access to food and clean clothes."

"But I can't leave."

"That depends on what we find."

She's already moving toward the door. I think maybe she'll turn around—say something human, something that acknowledges I'm a person and this is strange and she sees me sitting here in this room.

She pauses at the threshold.

"I've been doing this job for twenty-three years," she says. "Get comfortable."

Then she's gone.

The door closes. The lock clicks.

*Well fuck.*

The holding room is cleaner than the alley. Warmer. A bed with actual sheets, a dresser, a door that doesn't open from the inside.

Not a cell, they said.

Right.

Someone brought food—real food, more than I've eaten at once in months—and a change of clothes. Soft gray fabric. No House colors. The kind of thing you'd give someone who doesn't belong anywhere. I should laugh, but I can't find it in me.

I sit on the edge of the bed and stare at the wall.

This morning I woke up in an alley, hungry and cold and free. The same as every other morning for the last fifteen years. Invisible. Uncounted. Alive because no one was looking.

Now someone is looking. And I'm definitely not free.

The lights hum. Footsteps pass in the hallway. Voices I can't make out. Somewhere in this building, people are filling out forms about me. Making decisions about me.

I don't know what happens to people who don't have marks. I've spent my whole life making sure I never had to find out.

I lie back and stare at the ceiling.

Tomorrow they're going to examine me. Confirm what they already suspect. Try to figure out what I am.

And when they can't—

I close my eyes.

It's not like I'm going to fucking sleep anyway.

# Chapter 2
## Nova

I've been here for three fucking days.

I know because they keep replacing the food. Three trays a day—morning, midday, night. Nine trays I haven't touched. The headache started somewhere around tray five. The shaking started this morning, fine tremors in my hands that I can hide if I keep them pressed against my thighs or curled into fists.

The current tray is still there, sitting on the dresser where they left it. Bread and soup and something that might be meat, real meat, more food than I've eaten in weeks. The smell fills the room every time they bring a new one.

I don't touch it.

I've heard stories. Probably rumors, probably exaggerated, but I've survived this long by treating probably as definitely. Food makes you grateful. Food makes you compliant. Food makes you owe something to the people who gave it to you, and I don't plan on owing these people anything.

So I sit on the bed with my empty stomach and my shaking hands and I wait.

The lock clicks on the morning of the third day.

Same woman. Same folder. Same flat expression, like the seventy-two hours I've spent staring at these walls didn't happen at all.

"Come with me."

I stand. Too fast—my vision swimming for half a second before it clears. I lock my knees and follow her out.

The hallway is the same as before. Clean, bright, empty. Our footsteps echo. She doesn't look back to see if I'm keeping up, just walks like she expects me to follow, and I do, because what else am I going to do?

We pass the room where she asked me questions. Keep going. Through a door I didn't notice before, into a corridor that's colder, brighter, lined with doors that all look the same.

She stops at one of them. Opens it.

"Inside."

The examination room is white and chrome and cold enough that I feel it through the thin gray fabric they gave me. There's a table in the center, padded, with paper stretched across it. Cabinets along one wall. A counter with instruments I don't look at too closely.

A man is standing by the counter, writing something on a clipboard. He doesn't look up when I enter.

"Sit," he says.

I sit on the edge of the table. The paper crinkles under me.

The woman leaves. The door clicks shut. Just me and the physician now, and he still hasn't looked at my face.

"Name?"

"Nova."

"Age?"

"Twenty-six."

He writes it down. Flips a page.

"Hold out your hands."

I do. Palms up. He takes my left wrist without asking, turns it over, studies the inside where the mark should be. His fingers are cold and dry and clinical. He holds it for three seconds, maybe four, then drops it and takes the right one.

Same examination. Same nothing to find.

He makes a note.

"Lift your pant legs."

I bend down and roll the fabric up to my knees. He glances at the skin there—inside of the ankles, backs of the calves—and nods once.

"Stand and turn around. Lift your shirt."

I turn. Pull the gray fabric up to my shoulder blades. The air is cold on my bare skin. I stare at the wall and count my breaths while his eyes move across my back, looking for something that isn't there.

"Down."

I drop the shirt. Turn back around.

He's writing again. Hasn't said a word about what he found or didn't find. Hasn't looked at me once except to examine skin.

"No visible mark," he says to the clipboard. "Confirmed."

That's it.

He opens the door. The woman is waiting in the hallway.

"She's done," he says, and walks away.

The woman looks at me with the same flat expression she's had since the alley. "This way."

I follow her again. Different direction this time. The corridor curves, opens into a wider hallway with actual windows—first natural light I've seen in three days—and then stops at a door that looks different from the others. Warmer somehow. Less institutional.

She opens it.

"Wait here."

Then she's gone.

The room is small but not a cell. There's a chair that isn't bolted down, a small table, a window with actual light coming through it. No bed. No food tray. Just a space that feels like it's meant for people, not processing.

I sink into the chair because my legs are shaking and I'm not sure how much longer I can hide it.

Five minutes. Ten.

The door opens.

The woman who enters is not the same one. Different age, different build, different everything. She's maybe forty, with lines around her eyes that look like they come from expression, not exhaustion. She's carrying a cup of water and a blanket and she's looking at me.

Actually looking. At my face. Like I'm a person.

"I'm Linda," she says. "I'm sorry it took this long."

I don't say anything. I don't know what to say.

She sets the water on the table. Holds out the blanket.

"You're shaking," she says. Not an accusation. An observation. "You haven't eaten, have you?"

"I'm fine."

"You're not." She sits in a chair across from me. Doesn't push the water closer, doesn't insist on the blanket, just leaves them there. "Three days without food is not fine. I can see your hands trembling from here."

I curl my fingers into fists under the table.

"I'm not going to force you to eat," she says. "I'm not going to force you to do anything. But I need to tell you what happens next, and I'd rather do that when you're not about to pass out."

The water is right there. Clear and cold and probably not drugged, probably not a trap, probably just water.

I don't reach for it.

Linda watches me. I wait for the lecture about taking care of myself, the soft voice people use when they're about to make you do something for your own good.

"Okay," she says. "We'll do this your way."

She folds her hands on the table.

"We've had a team working on your case since you arrived. Searching for precedent—any record of someone your age without a mark. We couldn't find one. You're the first documented case of a permanent unmarked adult in the system."

I knew that already. I've always known that. Probably.

"The decision came down this morning. You're being transferred to the Academy."

The Academy. I've heard of it. Everyone's heard of it. The place where marks get confirmed, where House assignments get finalized, where people get sorted into the lives they're going to live.

I never thought I'd see the inside of it.

"There are three reasons," Linda continues. "First, you've never been through intake. The Academy is the standard process, even now. Second, there's some belief that the environment might increase the likelihood of manifestation. If there's a mark that hasn't surfaced yet, that's the most likely place for it to appear."

"Third." Linda pauses. "You've been flagged as part of a cluster."

The word means nothing to me.

She doesn't. Not immediately. Just watches me, like she's giving the word time to settle.

"What's a cluster?"

"A grouping. It happens sometimes—certain individuals show markers that suggest they should be grouped together. It's rare, but documented. You're showing those markers."

"Grouped with who?"

"A group at the Academy. Five men. They've been flagged for two years, but their cluster never finalized. The system thinks you're the missing piece."

I stare at her.

Five men. A cluster. Something that never finalized because I wasn't there.

"I don't know these people."

"I know."

"I didn't ask to be—"

"I know that too."

She says it simply. She doesn't get defensive about it.

"The transfer happens tomorrow. I wanted you to have time to understand before they move you."

"Understand what? That I'm being shipped off to live with strangers?"

"That you have more information now than you did an hour ago." Her voice is steady. "That's not nothing."

I want to argue. Want to tell her that information isn't the same as choice, that understanding doesn't mean accepting, that none of this is okay just because someone finally bothered to explain it.

But my head is pounding and my hands are shaking and I can feel the emptiness in my stomach like a living thing, and all I can manage is:

"Why do you care?"

Linda looks at me for a long moment.

"Because someone should," she says. "And because I've been doing this job long enough to know that how you treat people in the initial days determines everything that comes after."

She stands.

"The water isn't drugged. Neither is the food they've been bringing. I know you don't believe me, and I'm not asking you to. But when you're ready, it's there."

She moves toward the door. Pauses.

"I'll check on you before the transfer. If you have questions, I'll answer what I can."

Then she's gone.

The room is quiet. The light through the window is thin and gray.

I look at the water on the table. The blanket she left on the chair.

My hands are still shaking.

I don't reach for either one.

But I think about it.

That's new.

# Chapter 3
## LOCKE

Harrick's fist catches me across the jaw and I let it.

Not because I can't block it—I saw it coming from the moment he stepped into the corridor—but because taking the hit gives me the half-second I need to close the distance. His weight shifts wrong on the follow-through. Amateur mistake. I drive my knuckles into his ribs before he can reset, and the sound he makes is deeply satisfying.

"Fuck—"

His friend moves in from the left. I clock him without turning my head, already adjusting my stance, but before either of us can commit, a voice cuts through.

"That's enough."

Eli.

The group rounds the corner like they own the hallway. Five of them, moving together without thinking about it, the kind of easy coordination that comes from a cluster that actually finalized. Eli's at the front, one hand raised like he's directing traffic.

"Walk away, Harrick."

Harrick spits blood onto the floor. Looks at me, then at Eli, calculating odds he doesn't like.

"This isn't your business."

"It's not yours either." Eli's voice is bored. "And I don't feel like filling out incident reports today. Move."

For a second I think Harrick's going to push it. His jaw is tight, fists still clenched, pride warring with the math of five-on-two. Then his friend mutters something I can't hear and they're backing off, disappearing down the corridor with the kind of retreat that pretends it was always the plan.

Zoe catches my eye as her group passes. Holds it a beat longer than necessary. She doesn't say anything. Doesn't need to. The message is clear enough. *We handled it. You're welcome. Don't make us do it again.*

Then they're gone, moving together down the hall, and no one watches them go. Nobody whispers as they pass. Nobody stares. Just five people walking away like it's nothing, because for them it is nothing.

*Must be nice.*

I wait until the corridor is empty before I touch my jaw. Already swelling. Harrick hits harder than he used to, or maybe I'm just tired of getting hit.

The walk back to the house takes ten minutes. I use the time to settle my breathing, unclench my fists, get my shit under control. By the time I reach the front door, my hands are steady and my expression is flat.

Rane is in the kitchen when I come in. He looks up from whatever he's prepping, clocks my face, and sets down his knife.

"Harrick?"

"Harrick."

"How bad?"

"He'll piss blood for a week." I cross to the sink, run cold water over my knuckles. The skin's split across two of them, shallow but messy. "I'll live."

"You always do." He's watching me in that way he has, cataloging damage without making a production of it. "Someone step in?"

"Eli. His cluster with him. Sent him packing."

"Nice of them."

"It wasn't for us."

He doesn't argue. We both know how it works. They intervened because incidents cause paperwork, and paperwork draws attention, and attention is the last thing any finalized cluster wants. They didn't do it because they give a shit about us.

No one gives a shit about us.

I dry my hands on a towel and head for the common room. Kyron's on the couch with his phone, not even pretending to read it. He saw me come in. He sees everything.

"You're bleeding," he says.

"I'm aware."

"There's a kit under the bathroom sink."

"I know where the kit is."

I don't go get it. Instead I drop into the chair by the window and stare out at the courtyard. Empty path, flat light, nothing moving. Bonded housing—close enough to campus to be monitored, far enough to keep us separate from everyone else. Six clusters total, each of us tucked into our own little box where the system can watch us without the inconvenience of integration.

We're the only incomplete set. Have been for two years.

Two years of waiting for something that never came. Two years of being studied and monitored and quietly written off as a statistical anomaly. Two years of Harrick and people like him deciding that unfinished means broken, and broken means target practice.

Two years of knowing I'd take the hit for the right person without hesitation—and having no one to do that for.

I'm so fucking tired.

Beckett appears in the doorway. He takes one look at me—not at the blood, at *me*, reading something in my posture or my silence that I'm not aware I'm broadcasting—and disappears again. Returns a minute later with the medical kit. Sets it on the table beside me without comment.

He doesn't hover. Doesn't ask if I'm okay. Just makes sure I have what I need and settles into the armchair with a book he's probably already read twice. That's Beckett—always noticing, never pushing, waiting for the moment someone actually needs to be seen.

I wonder sometimes if he's as tired of waiting as I am.

I clean the cuts because it's easier than arguing.

Vaelor comes in an hour later, back from whatever training rotation he's been running. He smells like sweat and effort and something that might be optimism, which means he had a good session and hasn't heard about Harrick yet. He'll find out eventually. He always does.

"Food?" he asks the room.

"Already cooking," Rane calls from the kitchen.

"Need help?"

"When have I ever needed help?"

Vaelor ignores him and heads for the kitchen anyway. I hear them moving around each other, Vaelor pulling out plates before Rane can ask, Rane adjusting without breaking rhythm. Six plates. Always six.

This is normal. This is every day. The five of us in this house, moving around each other like we've been doing it for years—because we have—filling space that was designed for six and pretending the gap isn't there.

Except we don't pretend. Not really. We just don't talk about it.

Vaelor sets the sixth plate on the table like it's nothing. Like it doesn't mean anything. Like he hasn't done it every single night for two years, making space for someone who never showed up.

The notification comes at 7:43 PM.

I know the exact time because I'm looking at my phone when the message appears, and something in my chest cracks open before I even read the words.

*Cluster status updated. Missing element identified. Intake processing complete.*

I read it three times. The words don't change.

My hands are shaking. I don't know why. I'm not scared. I'm not relieved. I'm—

*Where the fuck have you been?*

The thought comes from nowhere, aimed at no one, and it doesn't make any sense. I don't know this person. I don't know anything about them. But something in my chest is *furious*—two years, two fucking years of waiting and fighting and carrying this space that was supposed to be filled, and now a message, now a notification, now *intake processing complete* like they've been sitting in some office somewhere while we—

I breathe. Force my hands flat on my thighs.

The common room has gone quiet. I look up and find four sets of eyes on me, because of course they noticed. Of course they felt the shift before I said anything. That's how it's always been with us—this awareness that isn't quite finalized, this almost-connection that the system has never been able to classify or complete.

"What?" Vaelor says.

I turn the phone around. Let them read it.

Silence.

Rane is the first to speak. "Missing element identified."

"That's what it says."

"So there's—" He stops. Starts again. "Someone's coming."

"Someone's already here." Kyron's voice is flat, but I can see him leaning forward slightly, that restless attention finally finding a target. "Intake processing complete. That means they've been in the system for at least a few days. Identified, located, processed. They were just waiting to notify us."

"Or waiting to make sure," Beckett says quietly. He's set his book down. I don't think I've ever seen him set a book down in the middle of a chapter before.

"Make sure of what?"

"That they had the right one."

The room settles into something that isn't quite silence.

Vaelor's still standing in the kitchen doorway, like he can't decide whether to come closer or give us space. The rest of them are just... waiting.

All of them looking at me.

And someone is about to walk into our lives and become part of whatever this nightmare is.

Two years.

And now a message that barely says anything. No name. No timeframe. Nothing usable.

*You're not incomplete anymore.*

"So," Rane says finally.

"So." I set my phone down. My knuckles are throbbing where the cuts are already starting to scab over. "They're late."

No one argues.

I stand up and the room shifts with me.

"I need air."

No one stops me.

The courtyard is empty this time of evening. The lights are starting to come on, artificial and too bright, casting everything in that flat institutional glow that makes shadows look wrong. I find a bench and sit and stare at nothing until the anger settles into something quieter.

Not gone. Never gone.

Just... waiting.

Someone is coming. Someone the system thinks belongs to us. Someone who's been processed and classified and scheduled for transfer like cargo, like a missing part finally located in a warehouse somewhere.

I don't know their name. I don't know anything about them.

But I already know I'd take a hit for them. I don't know why. I don't need to know why. The certainty is just *there*, sitting in my chest like it's been waiting for somewhere to land.

I stay on the bench until the lights finish coming on and the campus goes quiet and my hands stop wanting to form fists.

Then I go back inside.

The kitchen is clean. The food is put away. Five plates washed and stacked.

The sixth is still on the table.

Waiting.

# Chapter 4
## Nova

Linda comes in without a clipboard.

That's the first thing I notice—her hands are empty except for a small card she's turning over between her fingers. She looks tired, which is almost funny. She gets to go home every night. I've had three days of fluorescent lights and food I wouldn't touch. Well, four now.

"They're transferring you now," she says.

No preamble. No soft lead-in. I'm starting to appreciate that about her.

"Okay."

"Do you have any questions?"

I have a hundred questions. None of them are ones she can answer.

"Where am I going?"

"The Academy. I told you yesterday."

"I meant specifically."

"Cluster housing. You'll be assigned to the group I mentioned."

The five men. The incomplete set. The missing piece I'm apparently supposed to be.

"And if I don't want to go?"

Linda's expression doesn't change. "Then you'll be escorted instead of walked. The destination stays the same."

At least she's honest.

She sets the card on the table between us. Plain white, a name and a number printed in simple black text. No title. No department.

"If you're stuck," she says. "If something goes wrong. Call."

I look at the card. Look at her.

"Why?"

"Because someone should be paying attention." She stands. "And because I'd rather know than wonder."

She moves toward the door, and I realize she's not coming with me. This is goodbye—or whatever passes for it when you've known someone for a day and one of you is a prisoner.

"Linda."

She stops. Doesn't turn around.

"Thanks. For explaining."

"Don't thank me yet." She opens the door. "You haven't seen where you're going."

Then she's gone.

The system reasserts itself within minutes.

Two staff members I've never seen before appear in the doorway. Clipboards. Neutral expressions. The same flat institutional tone I've been hearing since the alley.

"Collect your belongings. You've been reassigned."

My belongings. The jacket I was wearing when they picked me up, still smelling faintly of the alley. The gray clothes they gave me. That's it.

I put on the jacket over the gray shirt. Slip Linda's card into the inside pocket where it won't fall out.

"Ready."

They don't respond. Just turn and walk, expecting me to follow.

I follow.

The transport is enclosed. No windows in the back, just a metal bench and a door that locks from the outside. I sit and count turns out of habit—left, right, straight for a long stretch, another left—but I'm not planning an escape route. There's nowhere to escape to.

If they wanted to hide me, they'd do it quietly. Back rooms. Unmarked vehicles. The kind of processing that happens where no one can see.

This is different. This is transport in daylight. Official transfer. Paperwork and procedure.

That means I'm being moved somewhere the system is willing to acknowledge.

I don't know if that's better or worse.

The transport slows, stops. The door opens from outside, and the light that floods in is different—brighter, cleaner. I step out, and the Academy is bigger than I expected.

I've heard about it my whole life—everyone has—but hearing about something and seeing it are different. The buildings are old, stone and glass, sprawling across grounds that look like they've been here longer than the territory itself. People move between them in clusters and pairs, talking, laughing, existing like this is normal.

Because for them it is.

And everywhere I look, I see marks.

Wrists bare and casual. Sleeves rolled up. House colors woven into clothing, displayed like they're supposed to be there. Because they are. Because that's what normal looks like.

I pull my sleeves down without thinking.

The escort moves me toward a security checkpoint near the main entrance. Scanners, badges, a desk staffed by someone who doesn't look up when I approach.

"Name?"

"Nova."

"Status?"

The escort answers for me. "Transfer. Provisional intake. Cluster assignment pending confirmation."

The woman at the desk types something. A badge prints out—temporary, the word VISITOR stamped across it in red—and she clips it to my jacket without asking.

"Proceed to orientation wing. Someone will meet you."

That's it. No explanation. No welcome.

I'm inside, but I'm not part of this place.

The difference is obvious.

The woman waiting for me at the end of the corridor looks like she belongs here.

She looks pleasant enough. It's the way she stands that gets me. She looks relaxed, like the ground beneath her feet has always been solid and always will be.

"Nova?" She steps forward with a small smile. "I'm Zoe. I'll be showing you around."

"Showing me around, or making sure I don't run?"

The smile doesn't waver. "Both, probably. But mostly the first one."

I almost like her for that.

"Come on," she says, turning toward the corridor. "It's a bit of a walk."

The Academy is a maze.

Hallways branch in every direction—training wings, administrative offices, residential buildings. Zoe points things out as we pass, her voice calm and informational.

"Dining hall's through there. Opens at six, closes at nine. Food's decent."

"Good to know."

"Training facilities are in the east wing. You probably won't have access to most of them yet."

"Yet?"

"Depends on your classification status." She glances at me sideways. "Which I'm guessing is complicated."

"You could say that."

She doesn't push. Just keeps walking.

We pass other students—groups of two and three, some alone, all of them moving with the easy confidence of people who know exactly where they're going. A few glance at us. At me. Their eyes catch on my temporary badge, my ill-fitting clothes, the way I'm scanning exits instead of looking straight ahead.

I'm not one of them.

They know it. I know it.

Zoe either doesn't notice or doesn't care.

We're cutting through a courtyard when it happens.

Footsteps behind us, quick and light. Zoe half-turns, and then there are arms around her waist, a body pressing close, lips brushing her temple.

"Hey."

The voice is male, warm, familiar in a way that has nothing to do with me. Zoe leans back into the embrace automatically, her whole posture softening.

"Hey yourself."

I look away. Then look back, because I can't help it.

He's tall, dark-haired, with the kind of easy confidence that comes from never having to question where you fit. His mark is visible on his wrist—I can't tell the House from here—and there's something else there too. A secondary mark, smaller. I don't recognize it.

"Who's your friend?" He's looking at me now, curious but not aggressive.

"She's new," Zoe says. "Being assigned to cluster housing."

His eyebrows lift. Just slightly. Just enough.

"Yeah?" He looks at me differently now—not suspicious, but aware. Like he's recalculating something. "Good luck."

Then he kisses Zoe's cheek, squeezes her once, and walks away.

Just like that.

They touched like it was nothing. Like it was easy. Like they'd done it a thousand times and would do it a thousand more.

"That's Eli," Zoe says, already moving again. "We finalized a few years ago."

She doesn't explain further. Doesn't offer context or reassurance or any of the things I'm not asking for anyway.

I follow her in silence.

Cluster housing is separate from the other students. Down a path lined with identical houses that look more like containment units than residences. Zoe stops in front of one of them—same as all the others, nothing to distinguish it.

"This is it," she says.

I stare at the door.

"They know you're coming," she adds. "I'll check on you tomorrow. If you need anything before then, there's a directory in the main hall."

"Thanks."

"Good luck, Nova."

That's twice someone's said that to me today. It's starting to feel less like a wish and more like a warning.

Zoe walks away without looking back.

I stand there for a long moment, staring at the door. Behind it are five people I've never met who are apparently supposed to be mine. Five strangers who've been waiting for me without knowing who I was.

Five men who probably have expectations I can't meet.

The system didn't ask me if I wanted this.

It never does.

# Chapter 5
## KYRON

The phone screen has gone dark twice and I keep tapping it awake without reading anything.

I'm in the chair by the window. Good light. That's the reason.

The others are scattered around the room, pretending to do things. No one's fooling anyone.

None of us are talking about it.

*Within the week*, the administrator said. Three days ago. She could show up in an hour or four more days and we have no way of knowing, so we're all just sitting here, waiting for our lives to change.

I look at my phone. Something about resonance signatures. I've read the same paragraph six times.

Then I feel it.

A pull. Low in my chest, like a hook catching on something I didn't know was there. I look up, out the window, and my hands go still.

Two figures on the path. Still far, just past the eastern quad. One walks like she knows exactly where she's going.

The other one is small. Silver-blonde hair catching the light.

I'm on my feet before I decide to stand. The phone hits the floor but I'm already at the glass, palm flat against it like I could reach through.

She's too far to see clearly. I can't make out her face, can't tell if she's scared or angry or calm.

It doesn't matter. My whole body already knows.

*Her.*

"Kyron?"

Rane's voice. I don't turn around.

"Kyron, what—"

"Window. Now."

I hear him get up. Cross the room. He stops beside me, follows my gaze.

"Holy shit." Barely a breath. "Is that—"

"Yeah."

"That's *her*?"

"Yeah."

And then they're all there. I don't know who moved first, but suddenly it's all five of us pressed against the glass like idiots, watching a woman we've never met walk up a path.

"She's early," Vaelor says. His voice is rough.

"She's here." I can't look away from her. "That's what matters."

She's closer now. I can see the way she holds herself—shoulders tight, drawn in. The way her head moves, scanning buildings like she's mapping exits. The way she stays behind the other woman instead of beside her.

"She's scared," Vaelor says quietly.

"She's careful," Beckett murmurs. "There's a difference."

"Is there?"

"Fear is reactive. That's not reactive. Look at how she moves."

I'm looking. I can't stop looking.

She's close enough now that I can see her face—pale, guarded, giving nothing away—and I'm already wondering what it would take to make her smile.

"You're staring," Beckett says.

"We're all staring."

"You're staring *differently*."

I don't have a comeback for that. He's not wrong.

"She's small," Rane says.

No one answers. I watch the way her steps land, deliberate and sure, no wasted movement. The way her clothes hang loose. The sharpness of her cheekbones. The shadows under her eyes.

She's been surviving. You can see it in every line of her.

"Something happened to her," Vaelor says.

Locke makes a sound. Low. Not a word.

I glance at him. His jaw is tight, eyes fixed on her, and there's something in his face I've never seen before. Something that makes me glad I'm not whoever hurt her.

"Locke," Rane says carefully.

"I'm fine."

He's not. None of us are. But he's the one who looks like he's about to put his fist through the glass.

She's almost to our walkway now. The woman beside her—Zoe—is gesturing at the building, explaining something. She nods, but I can tell she's not listening. Her eyes are moving. Cataloging. Assessing.

Smart. Careful. Alone for a long time.

I want to know everything about her. I want to know what she likes for breakfast and what makes her laugh and what her voice sounds like when she's not bracing for impact.

I want her to look at me.

"Kyron." Vaelor's voice, quiet. "Breathe."

Right. Breathing. That's a thing people do.

Zoe stops at the edge of our walkway. She's saying something—probably the standard orientation speech, here's where you'll be staying, here are the people you'll be living with, good luck with your new life that you didn't ask for.

Her shoulders tighten. I watch her take a breath. Steel herself.

Then Zoe turns and walks away, and the woman who's about to change everything is standing alone on the path, staring at our front door.

My hand is on the window frame. I don't remember putting it there.

"Someone should let her in," Rane says.

"Give her a second." Locke's voice is quiet. "She needs a second."

So we wait. Watch her stand there. Watch her make the decision to walk forward even though everything in her posture says she wants to run.

She doesn't run.

She walks to the door.

"I'll get it," Locke says, already moving.

Part of me wants to argue. Part of me is glad I don't have to be the first thing she sees. I don't trust my face right now.

The rest of us stay at the window like the lovesick idiots we apparently are.

I hear the door open. Locke's voice, low and even—I can't make out the words. A pause. Then her voice, and the sound of it hits me somewhere I wasn't ready for.

Soft. A little rough. Guarded but not weak.

I close my eyes for half a second just to get my shit together.

Footsteps. The door closing.

The air in the house changes.

She's inside. She's *here*. I can feel her like a physical thing—not just sound, not just presence, but something that slots into place in my chest like it's been waiting for exactly this space.

Rane exhales. "Okay. Okay. We can do this. We can be normal."

"Can we?" Vaelor's voice is strained.

"We have to. She's going to walk in here any second and see a group of guys who look like they've been hit by a truck. We need to pull it together."

He's right.

I turn away from the window. Force myself to breathe. Try to make my face look like something that won't terrify her.

The others scatter—trying to look like they weren't just plastered against a window. No one's pulling it off.

Footsteps in the hallway. Getting closer.

And then she's there.

Standing in the doorway. Silver-blonde hair and pale eyes and a face that's trying so hard to give nothing away.

Our eyes meet.

Everything *stops*.

My lungs forget how to work. My hands are shaking and I don't know when that started. The room narrows down to just her, just those pale eyes looking back at me, and everything I thought I knew about myself rewrites around a single thought.

*There you are.*

I'd know you anywhere. I'd know you in the dark, in a crowd, in a hundred years. I don't know how I know that but I do, I *do*, and she's standing right there and I can't—

She looks away first. Her cheeks go pink.

*Oh.* That blush. I want to know everything that makes her do that.

I take a step toward her without meaning to.

Rane's hand lands on my shoulder. Warm, solid, keeping me where I am.

"Easy," he murmurs, so low she can't hear.

Thank gods someone is stopping me from doing something stupid.

She's looking around the room now, taking in the space, the furniture, the four other men who are all trying very hard to look like they weren't just plastered against a window watching her walk up.

Her eyes come back to me.

Just for a second.

My chest does something stupid.

She almost smiles. *Almost.*

I'm going to spend the rest of my life trying to earn the full version of that smile.

Rane's hand tightens on my shoulder.

I still don't move.

I deserve a fucking medal.

# Chapter 6
## Nova

I reach for the door.

It opens before I touch it.

And my brain stops.

He fills the doorway. Tall—taller than me by almost a foot—with broad shoulders that block out the light behind him. Dark brown hair, green eyes that lock onto mine and don't let go. There's a bruise fading along his jaw, yellowing at the edges, and his knuckles are scraped raw.

He looks like he's been fighting. He looks like he won.

I forget to breathe.

He doesn't say anything. Just looks at me like—

I don't know. Like he's been waiting.

"I'm—" I have to clear my throat. "I'm Nova."

Something shifts in his expression. He steps back. Enough to let me through.

I'm suddenly very aware of how close I'll have to pass to get inside. How much space he takes up. The way his shoulders taper down to his waist in a sharp V.

I walk through the door and don't breathe until I'm past him.

The smell hits me first—something cooking, rich and warm, and my stomach cramps so hard I have to lock my knees.

Four days since I've eaten. Don't think about it.

Then the rest registers. Warmth. Lamplight. A space that feels lived-in.

I can feel him behind me. Locke. Every inch of where he's standing, like my body has decided to track him whether I want it to or not.

I step further into the room and there are more of them.

Four more.

My eyes catch on the one in the kitchen doorway first—impossible not to. He's the biggest person I've ever seen. Golden hair past his shoulders, arms that look like they could lift me without effort, chest straining against his shirt. He looks like a statue someone carved out of sunshine and then supersized. He's holding a glass of water, and there's a stillness to him that doesn't match his size at all.

"She's beautiful."

The words come from the couch, soft, like he didn't mean to say them out loud.

My head snaps toward him. Heat floods my face.

He's already blushing too. Auburn hair, warm eyes, and a face that's going red so fast I can almost watch it happen. His mouth opens like he's going to say something else, thinks better of it, and closes again.

Someone inhales sharply. Someone else mutters something and he says "Shut up" to no one in particular.

Great. Ten seconds and we've both made it weird.

"He's not wrong."

The voice comes from the window and I turn toward it and—

My mouth goes dry.

Blue.

That's it. That's the only thing in my head. Eyes so blue they hurt to look at, and I can't make myself stop. Dark hair, messy, falling into his face. Rings on his fingers. He's looking at me like he already knows something I don't.

I'm staring. I know I'm staring. I can't make myself stop.

He smirks.

My face goes hot again. I look at the floor.

"Ignore Kyron." The auburn one, still red. "He's like that with everyone."

"I'm not like anything."

"You're staring."

"I'm observing."

"There's really not a difference."

"There's a significant—"

"Do you want to sit down?"

The golden one. I turn too fast, overcorrect, have to catch my balance on nothing. He's moved closer—when did he move?—and he's holding out the glass of water. His hands aren't quite steady.

I notice. I don't know why I notice.

"She just got here." Locke, behind me. "Give her a second."

"I'm just—"

"Vaelor."

One word and the golden one stops. They're having a conversation I don't speak and I'm standing in the middle of it with my weight on the wrong foot.

"I'm fine." Too sharp. I hear it. Can't fix it. "I don't need to sit. I don't need water either."

I take a breath trying to calm myself but it's not working.

Nobody argues. Nobody looks away either.

Vaelor sets the water on the counter. I should say thank you or something but the words don't come.

"I'm Rane." The one on the couch. He's stayed where he is, giving me space. "That's Vaelor. Kyron's by the window—"

"Still staring," Kyron says.

"—still staring, and Beckett's in the chair."

I turn to find the last one and something in my chest goes quiet.

He's unexpected. Silver hair fading to pink, dark at the roots. Sharp cheekbones, dark brown eyes, tattoos covering his arms and disappearing under his sleeves.

He's the only one who isn't looking at me like I'm something to solve.

He leans forward in his chair and I take a step toward him without meaning to.

What the fuck am I doing?

I plant my feet, not willing to let it happen again.

I can breathe when I look at him.

He meets my eyes and I realize I've been standing here too long, looking at him too long, and the heat is back in my face and I need to—

"You already met Locke." Rane keeps talking like nothing happened. "He's friendlier than he looks."

"I'm really not," Locke says.

"He is. He just doesn't want anyone to know."

Locke makes a sound that might be disagreement but doesn't argue.

Rane's mouth twitches like he's won something.

"And you are…?" Rane prompts.

I blink. "What?"

"Your name."

"Oh." God. "Nova."

"Are you hungry, Nova?"

Vaelor again. The smell from the kitchen is making me dizzy. I press my hands flat against my thighs.

"I don't need anything."

Something passes between Vaelor and Rane. A look I can't read.

"Okay," Rane says. "Whenever you want it, there's always food in the fridge."

I nod without thinking.

I keep waiting for the pressure and it's not coming and I don't know what to do with my hands. Every time one of them moves I track it, all five, even when I'm only looking at one. My skin feels wrong. Too tight. And the only space to breathe is looking at Beckett.

*Since when? I need to get out of here.*

"Where do I sleep?"

It comes out harder than I meant. Rane doesn't react.

"Upstairs, down the hall. Third door on the left."

"It's been empty," Vaelor adds. "We can get you whatever you need—"

"She doesn't need the list right now." Kyron, still by the window. Still watching me with those impossible eyes. "She needs to breathe."

"I can breathe fine."

"You're not."

I want to argue but I can't because he's right. I've been holding my breath and now I have to let it out and they're all going to see.

"I'm tired." I make myself move. One foot. "Long day."

I walk past the couch. Past Vaelor, who steps back to let me through. Past the kitchen doorway that smells like food and makes my hands want to shake.

I glance back without meaning to.

They're all watching me go. Locke's hands are fists at his sides.

I walk faster.

Up the stairs, third door on the left. I close it behind me and lean back against the wood until my hands stop shaking.

*What the fuck was that?*

I couldn't think out there. Couldn't land on a single thought before the next one hit—my brain stopping at the door, staring at the one by the window, moving toward the silver-haired one like my body had its own plan.

That's not me. I don't do that.

This is adrenaline. It has to be.

I press my palms against my eyes until I see stars.

It doesn't help.

# Chapter 7
## BECKETT

She's gone and I haven't moved.

The hallway swallowed her up thirty seconds ago, maybe longer, and I'm still in the chair with my book closed on my lap like I'm waiting for something. I don't know what. Permission to breathe, maybe.

She stepped toward me.

I keep coming back to that. Not the way she looked—though that's there too, silver-blonde and pale-eyed and so thin it made something in my chest ache—but the way her weight shifted. Toward me. One step she didn't mean to take before she caught herself.

I've spent my whole life watching people. Learning what the small movements mean—the ones they don't know they're making. The way someone angles their body toward the door when they want to leave. The way hands curl into fists before a word gets said. The way eyes flick to the most dangerous person in a room, even when they're pretending not to notice.

She did that with Locke. Tracked him without looking. Flinched when Vaelor moved too fast. Went rigid when Kyron wouldn't stop staring.

But when she looked at me, her shoulders dropped.

I don't know what I did. I wasn't trying to do anything. I was just sitting here, not asking for anything, not pushing, and she—

I don't know. I don't know what happened.

What am I supposed to do with that?

"Well." Rane breaks first. Of course he does. "That went."

"Fantastically," Kyron says. Dry.

"I called her beautiful out loud. To her face. Within the first ten seconds."

"We know. We were there."

"I'm just saying, if we're ranking who made it weird—"

"You're winning," Locke says. "Congratulations."

Rane drops his head back against the couch. "She probably thinks we're insane."

"We are insane," Vaelor says from the kitchen doorway. He hasn't moved either. None of us have, really—just our mouths. "Did anyone else notice she didn't want to eat? Or drink? I offered her water and she looked at me like I was handing her a grenade."

"She's been in processing for days," Kyron says. "She doesn't trust anything with a label on it."

"It was a glass of water."

"From a stranger. In a house she didn't choose. After being transported here against her will." Kyron's voice is flat. "She's not wrong to be careful."

No one says anything.

I should say something. Contribute. I've been too quiet and they're going to notice, and then they're going to ask, and then I'm going to have to explain something I don't understand myself.

"Beckett."

*Too late.*

I look up. Rane is watching me, head tilted, something careful in his expression.

"You good?"

"Fine."

"You sure? You've got a look."

"What look?"

"The one where you're somewhere else entirely." He pauses. "Where'd you go?"

My face feels warm. I don't know why my face feels warm.

"It's stupid," I say.

"It's not," Rane says immediately. No hesitation.

He doesn't even know what I'm going to say. But that's Rane—he decides things before he has all the information.

"She moved toward me," I say, and my voice comes out too quiet. "Before she stopped herself."

Silence. I wait for someone to laugh, or shrug, or change the subject.

No one does.

"What do you mean?" Vaelor asks.

I look up. They're all actually listening.

"When you were introducing everyone. She looked at me and she—" I sit up a little straighter. "She took a step toward me. Then caught herself."

Rane sits up slowly. "I didn't see that."

"You were talking."

"I'm always talking."

"I know."

Kyron is watching me now with that sharp, assessing look he gets. I can feel it even without looking. "What do you think it means?"

"I don't know." My hands want to do something. I press them flat on the book. "She looked at me and her shoulders dropped. Just for a second. Like she could breathe."

No one says anything.

"And then she panicked," I add. "And left."

More silence. I'm definitely red now. I don't blush often but when I do it's obvious and I hate it.

Locke pushes off from the wall and moves toward the kitchen without a word. Vaelor steps aside to let him pass.

"Food," Vaelor says after a moment. "We should eat. It's ready."

It's a deflection and everyone knows it, but I'll take it anyway. Anything to move, to do something with my hands, So we can all stop standing around like idiots processing a five-minute interaction like it was a natural disaster.

Which it was. Sort of.

The kitchen is warm and smells like garlic and something roasted. Vaelor made enough for six—he always does now, has for weeks, like he's been preparing for her without admitting it. Plates come out. Silverware. The familiar rhythm of a meal we've shared a hundred times.

I take a plate. Put food on it. Sit at the table.

I don't taste any of it.

"She's going to be a problem," Rane says, and then corrects himself immediately. "Not like that. For our ability to function like normal humans."

"We've never functioned like normal humans," Kyron says.

"We've faked it better than this."

"Have we?"

"I didn't used to blurt out that women were beautiful the second they walked into a room."

"You absolutely did. You just didn't mean it before."

Rane opens his mouth. Closes it. "Okay, fair."

I push food around my plate. They keep talking—about her, about what happens next, about whether we're all going to survive this—and I'm listening but I'm not. Part of me is still in the living room, watching her step toward me and then away.

She didn't flinch when I looked at her. Everyone else made her flinch.

I don't know what to do with that.

Vaelor is cleaning up, moving plates to the sink, and I make a decision before I think about it too hard. I get up. Take a clean plate from the cabinet. Fill it carefully—enough to be a meal, not enough to overwhelm. The roasted vegetables. Some of the bread. A piece of the chicken.

"What are you doing?" Rane asks.

I don't answer. My face is warm again. I find the foil, cover the plate, find a marker in the drawer.

*Nova.*

I write it on a piece of tape and stick it to the foil. Open the fridge. Put the plate inside. Close the door.

When I turn around, they're all watching me.

My chest feels tight. "She didn't eat," I say. Too defensive. "She might later."

No one makes a joke. No one teases me about it. Vaelor just nods once, something soft in his expression, and goes back to the dishes.

I sit back down.

Maybe she won't even find it. Maybe she'll think it's weird. Some stranger making her a plate, putting her name on it like she's a kid at daycare. Maybe I should take it back out and pretend I never—

No. It's fine. It's just food. People need food.

My own plate is cold now. I eat it anyway.

We're halfway through cleanup when the alert comes through. All five of our phones buzz at once—that synchronized chime that means the system wants something.

Kyron checks his first. His expression doesn't change, but something in his posture tightens.

"Orientation," he says. "Tomorrow. 0900."

"All of us?" Rane asks.

"Cluster members required. Attendance mandatory."

"So yes."

Locke makes a sound. Low, irritated. "They're not wasting any time."

"They never do." Kyron sets his phone down. "They want to see how she fits. How we react to her. Whether we're stable."

"Are we?" Vaelor asks. It's not quite a joke.

No one answers.

I think about tomorrow. Nova in some bland room being walked through rules she didn't ask for. Us standing there pretending we're not cataloging her every breath.

We're not going to pass whatever test they're setting up.

I don't say that out loud.

The kitchen gets cleaned. Rane makes a bad joke about getting beauty sleep. Vaelor checks the fridge—checking on the plate, I realize, making sure it's still there. Kyron disappears to his room with his phone. Locke doesn't say goodnight; he never does.

I'm the last one in the kitchen.

The house is quiet now. Upstairs, behind the third door on the left, she's probably not sleeping. I'm not going to sleep either.

She stepped toward me.

I keep turning it over, trying to understand. I didn't reach for her. I didn't say anything soft or reassuring. I just sat there, existing.

And she moved toward me anyway.

I've watched people my whole life. I know what tension looks like, what fear looks like, what someone planning to run looks like. I know how to read a room before anyone says a word.

But I don't know how to read this. I don't know what it means when someone's shoulders drop just because they're looking at you.

I don't know how to be careful with something like that.

I turn off the kitchen light and go to bed.

# Chapter 8
## NOVA

I wake up and don't know where I am.

Ceiling. Why is there a ceiling. Why is it so dark. And the smell. It's wrong—clean, not damp, not concrete, not the alley.

Then it comes back. The house. The men. The way I couldn't think straight, couldn't stand straight, couldn't do anything except retreat to this room and press my back against the door until my hands stopped shaking.

I don't remember falling asleep.

That bothers me. I don't sleep like that. Not in new places, not around strangers, not when I don't know the exits or the locks or who might be listening. I lie awake for hours, days sometimes, until exhaustion drags me under against my will.

But I closed my eyes and then it was dark and now I'm awake and I don't know how much time I lost.

The clock on the dresser says 3:17.

The house is quiet. Not silent—there's the hum of something electrical, the faint tick of pipes cooling, the weight of a building settling into itself. But no footsteps. No voices. No movement.

My stomach cramps.

Four days. Almost five now. The smell from the kitchen earlier nearly dropped me, and I stood there refusing water like it was poison while my body screamed at me to take it, take anything, stop being so fucking stubborn—

*Whenever you want it, there's always food in the fridge.*

That's what he said. Rane. The one who called me beautiful and then turned red and told everyone else to shut up.

I lie there and listen to the house breathe.

They said I could. They said any time. That's not stealing. That's not owing anyone anything. They offered and I'm just... taking them up on it. Late. When no one's watching.

That's not weird.

That's fine.

I sit up slowly. My feet find the floor without sound. I'm still in the gray clothes they gave me at processing—I never changed, never even looked at the dresser to see if there was anything else. Why would there be, I don't belong no matter what their system says.

The door doesn't creak when I open it. I checked earlier, before I—before I fell asleep. Old habit. Know your exits, know your sounds, know what gives you away.

The hallway is dark. I keep one hand on the wall and move slowly, placing each foot before I shift my weight. The kitchen is at the end, past the living room where they were all sitting, watching me like I was something fragile and dangerous at the same time.

The living room is empty now. Just shapes in the dark—couch, chairs, the window where Kyron with those blue eyes stood and smirked when I couldn't stop staring.

I don't think about that.

The kitchen is darker than the hallway, but there's a light over the stove that someone left on, dim and orange. Enough to see by. I stop just inside the doorway and listen again.

Nothing.

The refrigerator is large and silver and hums quietly in the corner. I cross to it. Wrap my fingers around the handle. Hesitate.

*This is fine. They said I could.*

I open it.

The light inside is bright enough to make me squint. Shelves of food—real food, more than I've seen in one place in months. Containers and bottles and things wrapped in foil and—

My name.

There's a plate covered in foil with a piece of tape on top, and someone wrote my name on it in black marker.

*Nova.*

I stare at it.

I don't know what to do with this. Someone made me a plate. Someone covered it and labeled it and put it in the fridge for me to find, and I don't know who or why or what they expect in return. My mom used to…

My hands are shaking again.

I take the plate. Close the fridge. Stand there in the dim orange light holding food with my name on it and trying to remember how to breathe.

The bathroom. I can eat in the bathroom. Door locks, no windows, easy to clean up if I need to, and if someone wakes up I'm just—I'm in the bathroom. That's normal. That's not suspicious.

I move before I can talk myself out of it.

The bathroom is down the hall from my room. I passed it earlier. Small, clean, tile floor. I close the door behind me and lock it. Flip on the light. Sit down on the floor with my back against the tub.

The foil comes off easily. Underneath: roasted vegetables, bread, a piece of chicken. It's cold but it doesn't matter. Nothing has mattered less in my entire life than the temperature of this food.

I eat slowly.

Small bites. Chew until there's nothing left to chew. Swallow. Wait. Listen.

Another bite.

My stomach cramps around the first few bites, angry and confused after so long with nothing. I breathe through it. I've done this before—reintroducing food after a long stretch. You can't rush it. You take what your body can handle and you stop before you're full and you don't throw up, because throwing up wastes food and food is—

I stop that thought. I'm not in the alley. I'm not scrounging. There's a whole refrigerator twenty feet away and apparently people in this house make plates with my name on them.

I don't know what to do with that.

I eat half the plate and make myself stop. Wrap the rest back up. I'll figure out what to do with it later—hide it in my room, maybe, or put it back in the fridge, or—

The door opens.

The door opens. I thought I locked—

I freeze. Fork still in my hand, plate in my lap, caught in the bright bathroom light like an animal on the road.

Rane stands in the doorway.

He's wearing a t-shirt and shorts and his hair is messed up from sleep and he freezes too, one hand still on the door, eyes going wide as he takes in the scene—me on the floor, the plate, the foil, my face.

One second. Two.

I can't move. Can't speak. Can't do anything except sit here and wait for whatever comes next.

His expression shifts. The surprise fades into something else that I don't understand. He doesn't look at the plate again. Doesn't look at how I'm sitting on the bathroom floor at 3am eating in secret like a feral animal.

"Sorry," he says. Quiet. "Didn't know anyone was in here."

I still can't speak.

He nods once. "Take your time."

Then he steps back and closes the door behind him.

I sit there for a long moment, heart pounding, waiting for the knock, the questions, the check-in to make sure I'm okay. Waiting for him to tell someone, to make it into something, to turn this into a conversation I don't know how to have.

Nothing.

Footsteps moving away. A door closing somewhere else in the house.

That's it.

I look down at the plate in my lap. Half-eaten, my name still on the foil in black marker.

He saw. He knows. And he just... left.

I don't know why that makes it worse.

I get up, rinse the fork and head back to the kitchen. I open the fridge and shove the plate toward the back where it's not the first thing someone sees. I shut the door and stand there in the dark for a second, listening.

Nothing.

I go back to my room, closing the door behind me.

As I lay down, I realize I keep waiting to feel something—shame, maybe, or anger, or the sick twist of being caught doing something wrong. But all I feel is the food settling in my stomach for the first time in days.

He didn't make it into anything.

He just let me have it.

I stare at the ceiling and know that I still won't sleep, but this time it's not because I'm scared.

I don't know what it is.

# Chapter 9
## NOVA

Morning light is too bright.

I don't know when I finally fell asleep, but it wasn't for long. My body feels heavy and wrong, like I'm moving through water. But there's noise in the house—voices, footsteps, the clatter of something in the kitchen—and I can't hide in this room forever.

I sit up. Look at the dresser I ignored last night.

Might as well.

The drawers have clothes in them. Nothing fancy, but they're clean and soft and roughly my size. Someone put these here. Someone thought about what I might need before I arrived.

I'm not sure how I feel about that.

I pull on a pair of gray joggers and a black t-shirt that's a little too big but not swimming on me. They're better than the processing clothes. Better than anything I've worn in a long time, if I'm being honest.

The hallway is bright. Sunlight through windows makes the house looks different—warmer, more lived-in. Less like a trap.

I make myself walk toward the noise.

The kitchen is full of them.

They're all here, moving around each other with the easy rhythm of people who've done this a thousand times. Someone's saying something about a training schedule. Vaelor is at the counter, doing something with the coffee maker. There's a conversation happening that I walked into the middle of.

Rane is at the table.

He looks up when I enter. Our eyes meet.

My chest tightens. Here it comes. The question, the comment, the acknowledgment of what he saw last night—

He gives me a small smile. "Morning."

That's it.

He goes back to his phone. No mention of the bathroom. No mention of me on the floor with a plate in my lap at 3am. Nothing.

Why would he do that?

"How'd you sleep?" Vaelor asks, not turning from the counter.

I hesitate. "Fine."

"Liar," Kyron says, almost amused. He's pouring coffee. "No one sleeps the first night."

"Kyron didn't sleep for three days when he got here," Rane offers. "Just sat in the corner like a suspicious cat."

"That's not—" Kyron stops. "Okay, that's mostly accurate."

"I slept fine," Locke says.

"You sleep like the dead," Rane says. "It's unsettling."

"There's food," Vaelor says, gesturing to the counter. "Help yourself. Donuts, or I can make eggs if you want something real."

I look. A box of donuts that smells heavenly. Not just that, but it's something I can take with me if I need to leave.

"Donut's fine." I take one with colored sprinkles. Hold it in my hand without eating it yet.

Vaelor sets a mug of coffee in front of me. Black. I set the donut down and wrap my hands around the cup because it's warm and I don't know what else to do with them.

I stare at it.

"I've never actually..." I stop.

"You've never had coffee?" Rane looks genuinely wounded. "Ever?"

"It wasn't exactly a priority."

"Damn." He shakes his head. "Okay. Sip it. Tell us what you think."

I take a sip. Try not to make a face. Fail.

"Too bitter?" Vaelor asks.

"Little bit."

He takes the mug back without comment, dumps half of it, adds something from the fridge. Slides it back to me.

I try again. Not great, but drinkable.

Vaelor watches me. "Better?"

"Yeah."

"We'll figure it out," he says, and turns back to the stove.

No one watches or comments. I let myself relax just a little.

Beckett comes in from the hallway, still looking half-asleep. He makes a straight line for the coffee without acknowledging anyone, pours a cup, and leans against the counter with his eyes closed.

"He's not a person until the second cup," Rane says to me, like he's sharing a secret.

Beckett raises a middle finger without opening his eyes.

A giggle escapes before I can stop it. Small, surprised. I clamp my mouth shut.

Locke glances at me. Something flickers across his face—not a smile, but close. He looks away before I can say anything.

"Did you get the text about orientation?" Rane asks.

"What text?"

"They sent it last night. Nine o'clock this morning."

"I don't have a phone."

The room pauses. Vaelor and Rane exchange a look.

"We'll fix that," Kyron says.

"I don't need—"

"You do." He's looking right at me. "We need to be able to communicate. All of us."

I want to argue. I want to tell him I've survived fifteen years without a phone, without anyone needing to reach me, without being part of anyone's "all of us."

But the way he says it makes the argument die in my throat.

I shut my mouth.

"Orientation is mostly procedural," Rane says. "Rules, expectations, schedule stuff. Boring."

"They'll ask questions," Locke adds. "About you. About us. About how the cluster is adjusting."

"What do I say?"

"As little as possible."

"If it gets uncomfortable, we're there," Beckett says. "All of us. Same room."

I look at him. Remember the way I stepped toward him last night without meaning to. The way I could breathe when I looked at him.

He meets my eyes for a second, then looks away.

"And if something goes wrong?" I ask.

"Then we'll be right there when it does," Rane says.

I don't think that's as reassuring as he thinks it is.

I eat the donut standing up, taking small bites. They talk around me—about the schedule, about someone named Harrick, about things I don't understand yet. I let it wash over me without trying to track it all.

At 8:40, they're moving toward the door before anyone says it's time to go. I'm two steps behind before I realize I'm following.

The walk to orientation is strange.

I don't notice it at first—I'm too busy looking at the campus in daylight, the buildings and paths and people moving between them. But after a few minutes, something feels off.

They've gravitated around me. Locke slightly ahead, Vaelor somewhere behind, the others filling in the gaps. Adjusting their pace to match mine without seeming to think about it.

I've always been separate. I've never been part of something. I'm not sure what I'm feeling, but I'm not mad about it.

We round a corner and I feel it before I see it.

The air changes. My body tightens before my brain catches up—that instinct that says *wrong wrong wrong* even if I don't know why.

Locke shifts and I'm looking at three men on the path ahead. One makes eye contact that gives me the ick. They're waiting for us.

My group slows.

"Harrick," Locke says. Low. He's not happy to see them.

The one in front—tall, broad, dark hair slicked back—smiles. It doesn't reach his eyes.

"Heard you finally got your missing piece." His gaze slides past Locke, past Kyron, and lands on me. "This her?"

No one answers.

Harrick tilts his head, looking me over like I'm something he found on the ground. "Huh. Not what I expected."

*What the fuck?*

"Walk away," Locke says.

"Just saying hello." Harrick's smile widens. "Being neighborly."

I watch it happen like it's in slow motion.

Kyron shifts his weight. Beckett steps forward—not in front of me, but beside me, close enough that I feel the heat of him. Vaelor moves from behind me to my left, blocking the angle. Rane goes still in a way I haven't seen from him before.

And Locke—

Locke doesn't move at all. But something in him changes. Something in the air around him goes cold and heavy, like the space itself is holding its breath.

"I said walk away."

The words are quiet. Flat. Final.

Harrick's group shifts. One of them mutters something. Another takes a half-step back.

Harrick holds Locke's gaze for a long moment. Then he laughs—short, dismissive—and shrugs.

"Fine. See you around, new girl."

They walk past us. One of them shoulders close enough that I feel the air move, and Beckett's hand twitches at his side but doesn't rise.

Then they're gone.

I realize I'm not breathing. I force myself to inhale.

No one says anything. They just start walking again, like nothing happened.

But something did happen. I don't know what, but I can feel it in my bones. A shiver runs down my spine, but it's not from fear.

That's a problem.

Why aren't I afraid of what I just saw? I'm oddly calm and that doesn't feel right. But it also feels more right than anything I've ever felt.

That scares me more than Harrick ever could.

The Academy building looms ahead, stone and glass and windows that catch the morning light. People stream in and out, normal and unbothered, like the world didn't just tilt sideways on the path behind us.

We walk through the doors.

Whatever comes next, I'm not facing it alone.

I don't know if that makes it better or worse.

# Chapter 10
## Nova

Whatever I was expecting, this isn't it.

One row of chairs facing a podium. Six seats in a line, like we're waiting to be processed.

I move to take a seat and notice another chair in the back corner. I don't know why that bothers me, why there's a tightness in my chest that showed up as soon as I saw it. I take a breath and sit.

The guys settle around me without discussion. I end up between Rane and Beckett. Locke takes the end closest to the door.

The woman at the front waits until we're seated. She has a tablet in her hands and an expression that gives nothing away.

"This session is mandatory for all provisional clusters," she says. "Attendance is recorded. You will remain seated unless directed otherwise."

She looks down at her tablet.

"This group has been designated for review due to its unique forming sequence."

She looks at all of us.

"Four years ago, five individuals affiliated with separate Houses were identified as repeatedly congregating within a restricted radius. Contact occurred in variable configurations. One or two at a time. No fixed hierarchy."

She says it like she's reading a weather report.

"Relationships formed prior to system intervention."

I feel Beckett shift beside me. Barely. Like he knows exactly where this is going.

"After two years of persistent co-location and unauthorized proximity, the system identified a cluster. Due to the individuals' relevance within their respective Houses, the cluster was placed under elevated observation."

She looks up. Scans the row. Her eyes pass over me like I shouldn't be here.

"The cluster was assigned a high-threat designation."

High-threat. These five men sitting in a row of chairs, not moving, barely breathing.

*What the fuck?*

She looks back at her tablet.

"Separately."

The word hangs there.

"An individual was recorded as lost outside of the system at age eleven following the confirmed deaths of her parents."

My parents. She's talking about my parents. My hands curl into fists in my lap.

"The system classified the subject as an anomaly. The anomaly was tracked intermittently across multiple House territories over a fifteen-year period."

Fifteen years. Tracked. They knew where I was. They always knew.

"The anomaly was located and capt—"

She stops. Glances at her tablet.

"—brought in for intake."

The door opens.

A guy steps in, already looking like he's in the wrong place.

"No House marking was identified."

His eyes snap to the trainer. Just for a second. Then he's stepping back, hand on the door.

"Sorry—wrong room."

Tall. Sandy hair. Broad shoulders. Moving like he wants to disappear.

But as he's turning to leave, he looks up.

Our eyes meet.

Something happens. Because right now, there's no one else in this room. The air gets heavier, or my chest gets tighter, or the world exploded and I don't know. I just know that something that was fine a second ago isn't fine anymore.

Someone behind me mutters something. It sounds like "fuck."

The trainer doesn't react to the interruption. Same voice. Same cadence.

"Excuse me. Can I get your name?"

The guy blinks. He was leaving. Now he's not.

"Trey," he says. "I was looking for—"

"House?"

"Dream. Originally." He hesitates. "I have Memory markers too. It's complicated."

"Assignment?"

"Training rotation B. Room 114."

"This is 114."

Trey looks at the door. Looks at the number on the wall. Something in his face shifts—confusion becoming something else.

"That's... not right."

One of the guys says, very low, "No."

The trainer makes a note on her tablet.

Her expression doesn't change. "Please take a seat. We'll need to verify a few things before you proceed."

Trey hesitates then moves across the room. Toward the empty chair in the back. He looks at the guys like he's trying to figure out what he walked into.

He sits, and I feel his eyes on me.

"We'll proceed slightly differently this morning," the trainer says. "There are additional protocols to address."

That doesn't sound like a choice.

I glance at Beckett. He's staring at his hands like he's holding them still on purpose.

Whatever just happened, they felt it too.

And none of them are happy about it.

# Chapter 11
## VAELOR

I can't stop thinking about the door.

It's been hours. Training ended. I showered, changed, started prepping dinner like I always do. Normal things. Routine things. But my hands keep pausing mid-motion, and I'm back in that room watching it happen again.

The door opening. The trainer not stopping. Trey's eyes snapping to her when she said it.

*No House marking was identified.*

I set down the knife and stare at the cutting board.

No House marking. I keep turning that over, waiting for it to make sense.

I've seen the archives. Memory keeps records going back centuries—every birth, every bond, every formation. First mark appears at birth. Always. That's not policy, that's biology. The mark shows up because the system claims you.

So what happens when it doesn't?

There are a handful of documented cases over the centuries—late bloomers, a few faded marks, one or two unusual placements. Rare enough to warrant their own archive sections. But no mark at all?

I've got nothing.

Which means either there's a gap in the archives that Memory House somehow missed for centuries, or Nova is the first person this has ever happened to.

Neither answer makes sense. Neither answer helps.

And then there's the timing.

Memory doesn't believe in coincidence. Memory believes in sequence. And that sequence was too clean to be an accident.

The kitchen is quiet. Kyron passed through twenty minutes ago, grabbed water, said nothing. He's been like that all afternoon—watching things instead of people, which means he's processing something he doesn't want to talk about yet. Locke hasn't spoken more than ten words since we got back. Beckett's been in the armchair with a book he hasn't turned a page of.

No one's said the word "orientation."

At some point, we're going to have to. I know that. We can't just keep circling each other, pretending the room didn't shift under our feet this morning. But no one wants to be the one to start. No one wants to say it out loud and make it real.

I go back to chopping vegetables. Muscle memory. Something to do with my hands while my brain keeps circling.

\* \* \*

Rane finds me on the back steps an hour before dinner.

I'm not hiding, I don't think.

I'm just sitting, watching the light change, trying to settle something that won't settle. He drops down beside me without asking.

"You've got to be fucking kidding me."

I don't answer. I already know what he's going to say.

"You think that was real?" he asks. "You think that actually meant something?"

"I think it was a mistake."

"A coincidence."

I give him a look.

"Seriously?" He runs a hand through his hair. "That's what we're going with?"

"What else do you want to call it?"

"It took them two years to even identify us as a potential cluster." He's leaning forward now, elbows on his knees. "Two years of us showing up in the same places, two years of whatever the hell this is, and they barely noticed. You really think one wrong entrance is going to set off alarms?"

I stop looking at the sky. Look at him instead.

"Yes."

He blinks. "Yes?"

"Yes. I do."

The silence stretches. Rane's waiting for me to explain, and I don't want to, because saying it out loud makes it real.

"They took two years to notice us," I say, "because they didn't want to. We were inconvenient. Complicated. Easier to file under 'anomaly' and wait for it to resolve itself."

"So?"

"So they noticed him immediately." I keep my voice even. "He walked through a door and they stopped mid-sentence to ask his name. That's not protocol. That's not procedure. That's the system paying attention."

Rane's quiet for a long moment.

"You're saying the timing matters."

"I'm saying the timing is the only thing that matters." I look back at the sky. "He didn't just walk into the wrong room. He walked in at the exact moment she was being named as unmarked. That's not coincidence. That's overlap."

"Overlap with what?"

"I don't know yet."

He doesn't like that answer. I can feel him wanting to argue, wanting to find the hole in the logic, the reason this doesn't mean what I think it means.

"Maybe it's nothing," he says finally. "Maybe he's just some guy with a scheduling error."

"Maybe."

"But you don't think so."

"No." I stand up, brushing off my pants. "I don't."

Dinner is quiet.

I made enough for six, like I always do. Habit at this point. The extra portion sits on the counter, covered, waiting for someone who isn't here yet.

Nova comes to the table last. She's been in her room since we got back—not hiding, exactly, but not present either. She looks tired in a way that has nothing to do with sleep.

She sits between Rane and Beckett. Same configuration as this morning, like it's already become muscle memory.

I watch her look at the food.

It's subtle. If I weren't paying attention, I'd miss it. But I am paying attention, so I see everything.

The way her eyes move across the dishes before she reaches for anything. The way she waits until someone else serves themselves first. The way she takes small portions, careful portions, like she's calculating something I can't see.

She eats slowly. Controlled. Stops before her plate is empty.

No one comments. No one pushes seconds on her. The guys have figured out, without discussing it, that pressure makes it worse.

But I notice when she reaches for the bread. The way her hand hesitates for just a fraction of a second, like she's checking to make sure it's allowed. Like she's waiting for someone to tell her no.

Fifteen years. That's what the trainer said. Fifteen years outside the system.

I don't know what that looks like. I don't know what kind of life teaches you to reach for bread like it might disappear. But I'm starting to understand that whatever happened to her didn't just happen once. It happened every day, for years, until it became the shape of her.

I get up to refill the water pitcher. When I come back, I set a small plate of rolls closer to her side of the table. Not offering. Not commenting. Just making them easier to reach.

She doesn't look at me. But she takes one.

After dinner, she disappears upstairs.

I start on the dishes. Beckett brings his plate over without being asked, sets it on the counter beside me.

"You're out of dish soap," he says.

"There's more under the sink."

"Found it."

He hands me the bottle. That's it. That's the whole conversation. But he stays in the kitchen instead of going back to his chair, which means he doesn't want to be alone with whatever he's thinking.

Rane's voice drifts in from the other room. "—didn't even finish the orientation. Just said 'additional protocols' and dismissed us."

"She'll reschedule," Kyron says. Flat. Uninterested.

"Will she though? Because that felt pretty final."

"It wasn't final. It was interrupted."

"Same difference."

"It's really not."

I rinse a plate and set it in the rack. The conversation isn't about orientation. It's about not talking about Trey, not talking about Nova, not talking about the fact that everything shifted today and none of us know what to do with it.

Locke hasn't said a word. He's by the window, jaw tight, watching the path outside like he's expecting someone. Beckett's book is closed on the armchair. Rane's being too loud about nothing, which means he's scared.

And Nova is upstairs, alone, with whatever she's carrying.

I dry my hands on the towel and hang it on the hook.

Tomorrow isn't about orientation anymore. Tomorrow is about what the system does next.

And I don't think any of us are ready for it.

# Chapter 12
## NOVA

I wake up to voices downstairs.

Not loud—just the sounds of people existing in the same space. Cabinets opening. Water running. Someone laughing at something someone else said.

I lie there for a minute, letting it wash over me. They sound like a family down there. They've had years to become this, to learn each other's rhythms and jokes and silences. And now I'm here, dropped into the middle of something that was already whole.

I shove that thought down and move.

I pull on the same gray joggers from yesterday and a clean shirt from the dresser, run my fingers through my hair. Good enough.

The kitchen is warm and smells like coffee and eggs.

"—can swap with Rane for third period, that covers Resonance Studies."

"And fourth?"

"Vaelor's got House History."

"That leaves Mark Theory."

Silence falls over the room.

"None of us have Mark Theory."

I stop in the doorway. Kyron's got his phone out, frowning at it while Rane leans over his shoulder. They're both staring at something on the screen like it personally offended them.

"We could talk to the registrar," Rane says. "Switch something around."

"They're not going to let us rearrange our schedules because we don't like hers."

"We could ask."

"We could also not look like obsessive psychopaths."

Locke clears his throat. Loud. Pointed. "Too late for that."

Kyron looks up. Sees me in the doorway. His expression flickers for just a second, and then the phone disappears behind his back like a kid caught with something he shouldn't have.

"Morning," he says. Too bright. Not at all suspicious.

Rane spins around so fast he almost knocks over his coffee. "Hey! You're up. That's great. We were just—" He looks at Kyron. Kyron looks at the ceiling. "—talking about the weather."

"The weather," I repeat.

"It's supposed to rain."

"It's not," Vaelor says from the stove without turning around.

"It might."

"There's not a cloud in the sky."

"Weather changes, Vaelor."

I lean against the doorframe. "Were you talking about my schedule?"

Silence. And suddenly everyone finds something else to look at.

"Because it sounded like you were talking about my schedule."

Rane opens his mouth. Closes it. Opens it again. "Okay, yes. But in a totally normal, not-at-all-creepy way."

"You literally just said you were being obsessive psychopaths."

"I said we could *also* not look like that. Implying we weren't already."

"That's not what that implied."

Kyron sighs and pulls the phone back out. "We were making sure you had one of us in your classes. That's all."

"Why?"

He looks at me like the answer should be obvious. "Because you don't know anyone. And after yesterday with Harrick, people are going to—"

"Kyron." Locke's voice is low, cutting across the room in warning.

Kyron stops. His jaw tightens but he doesn't finish the sentence.

"It's your first day," Rane says, stepping in. "We just wanted to make sure you weren't alone. That's all."

"Uh, yeah, thanks," I say trying not to sound awkward.

I try to focus on breathing, but with the five of them, all in the same room, all looking at me it feels impossible. My skin feels too tight again, that same prickling awareness I had yesterday.

*Fuck.*

The fridge opens beside me and Beckett holds out a glass of orange juice without comment. "Morning."

I take it because he's already pressing it into my hand. "Morning."

He moves past me toward the table and I catch Vaelor watching me from the stove. Not the food. Me. When our eyes meet, he looks away too fast, turning back to the eggs like they suddenly need all his attention.

My face feels warm. I focus on the orange juice.

"Breakfast," Vaelor says, and suddenly everyone's moving.

Plates come out of cabinets while Rane grabs silverware and Kyron sets down his phone to help. Someone puts toast on a plate and hands it to someone else who hands it to me. Beckett pulls out a chair and Locke pushes off the wall to take a seat.

I blink and somehow I'm sitting at the table with a full plate in front of me.

*What the fuck just happened?*

They're already eating, already talking about something else, and I'm still trying to figure out how I got here. I pick up my fork and take a bite without really tasting it.

By the time Kyron stands and grabs his bag, my plate is half empty and I don't remember eating any of it.

"We should go," he says. "Don't want to be late."

I grab my schedule and follow him out.

The day is exactly what they promised. Every class, one of them is there. Kyron in Territorial Protocol, catching my eye when I get lost and mouthing "later" like he's already planning our study session. Rane in House History, whispering commentary until the professor glares us into silence. Vaelor in Resonance Studies, a wall of calm between me and everyone else.

And everywhere—the staring. The whispers. Eyes tracking me like I'm something dangerous, something wrong, something that doesn't belong. I keep my head down and try to focus on the lectures, but I understand maybe half of what's being said. Fifteen years is a lot to miss.

By the end of the day, I'm exhausted and my skin still prickles every time one of them gets too close. Rane's shoulder bumping mine in the hallway. Vaelor's hand on my back, guiding me through a door. Kyron leaning in to say something, his breath warm against my ear.

I don't know what my body is doing. I'm choosing not to think about it.

When the last class before Mark Theory ends, it's Beckett waiting outside the door.

"One more," he says.

We walk. He doesn't fill the silence, and I'm grateful for it. Almost like I can just exist, and that feels oddly nice.

"This is you," he says stopping in front of the marked doorway. "Mark Theory."

The cold feeling from this morning settles back into my stomach.

"None of you are in this one."

"No." He pauses. "But we'll be right here when you get out."

I nod. He doesn't move, like he's waiting for something.

"I'll be fine," I say, even though I'm not sure that's true.

"I know." He says it like he believes it. "You've got this."

I nod, heading inside.

The room is small. Twelve chairs arranged in a circle with no desks, nothing between me and the other students. It feels intimate in a way that makes my skin crawl.

I take a seat near the door and count the other students as they filter in. Eight. Nine. Ten.

The professor is a woman with gray hair and sharp eyes. She's arranging papers on a small table in the center of the circle.

Two empty seats remain. The door stays open.

I'm starting to think I might actually survive this when it opens one more time.

Two people walk in together.

Trey.

My chest tightens before I can stop it. His eyes find mine now and there it is again, that same pull, I felt in orientation.

And beside him, a man with dark hair, cold eyes. One of Harrick's group from the path yesterday. He doesn't look away when our eyes meet, and I don't like it.

They cross the room and take the last two seats. Directly across from me.

The door clicks shut.

Oh shit.

# Chapter 13
## Nova

The professor waits until the door clicks shut, then looks around the circle.

"Mark Theory is not a lecture course," she says. "It's a discussion. You will be expected to participate, to share, and to examine your own experiences alongside the texts."

Great. My favorite kind of class. The kind where I can't hide.

"We'll begin with introductions. Name and mark. Show your wrist as you speak." She gestures to the student on her left. "We'll go clockwise."

My stomach drops. I count the seats between that student and me. Seven people. Seven introductions before I have to figure out what the hell to say.

The first student extends her wrist. A clean mark, elegant lines. "Sera. Dream."

The next. "Jonah. Shadow."

They go around. I stop listening to the names and start planning my escape. I could say I'm sick. I could say I need the bathroom. I could just stand up and walk out and never come back.

Five people left.

Four.

Three.

The girl next to me finishes. "Lira. Whisper."

Everyone looks at me.

I don't move.

"Your name?" the professor prompts.

"Nova." My voice comes out steadier than I feel. "I don't—"

I stop. The words won't come. I don't have a mark. I've never had a mark. I'm the anomaly, the glitch, the thing the system doesn't have a name for.

I start to stand.

"Miss Wilder." The professor's voice is calm. "The faculty has been briefed on your situation. Please, sit down."

The room is silent. I can feel everyone staring, but it's two sets of eyes that burn the most. Trey, watching me with something I can't read. And Harrick's friend, watching me like I just confirmed something he suspected.

I sit.

My hands are shaking. I extend my wrist anyway, showing them nothing. Bare skin where a mark should be.

Someone inhales sharply. Someone else shifts in their seat. The professor just nods and moves on.

"Next."

The introductions continue. I'm not breathing. I'm counting the remaining students, waiting for it to be over, when—

"Trey."

I look up.

He extends his wrist and I see it—two patterns overlapping, bleeding into each other, neither one complete. Dream and Memory tangled together in a way that looks almost painful.

"I couldn't figure out who I wanted to be," he says.

He's looking at me when he says it.

The words light up something inside me. I don't look away. I can't.

The moment stretches. Then he drops his wrist and the professor moves on.

"Silas. Shadow."

Harrick's friend. Silas. I file the name away and watch him extend his wrist. Clean mark, sharp lines. Nothing abnormal.

But when his eyes meet mine, he smiles. Just a little. Just enough to make my skin crawl.

The introductions end. The professor starts talking about mark inheritance, activation sequences, the factors that influence when and how a mark manifests. Every word feels like it's aimed directly at me.

I try to take notes. I try to focus. But I keep feeling Trey's eyes drifting back to me, and Silas's smile, and the weight of that bare wrist everyone just saw.

By the time class ends, I'm wound so tight I might shatter.

The professor dismisses us and I'm out of my chair before she finishes speaking, heading for the door, needing to get out of this room and away from the circle and the staring and—

"Nova."

Trey's voice. Low. Behind me.

I stop. I don't know why I stop.

He catches up to me in the hallway, and for a second we just stand there. He's taller than I remembered. Broader. His eyes are gray and searching and I don't know what he's looking for.

"I just wanted to say—" He stops. Runs a hand through his hair. "That was shit. What she made you do. I'm sorry."

I don't know what to do with an apology I didn't ask for.

"It's fine," I say.

"It's not." He says it simply, like it's obvious. "But okay."

There's a pause. He's still looking at me like he wants to say something else, and I'm still standing here like an idiot, and I don't understand why I haven't walked away yet.

"Trey." Silas's voice cuts through the moment. He's in the doorway, watching us. "You coming?"

Trey's jaw tightens. Just for a second. "Yeah."

He looks at me one more time. "I'll see you around, Nova."

Then he's gone, walking toward Silas, and I'm left standing in the hallway trying to figure out what just happened.

I find the exit. Push through the doors into the afternoon light.

The guys are waiting. All five of them, spread across the steps like they've been there the whole time. Beckett sees me first and straightens. Then they're all looking, all reading whatever's on my face.

"How bad?" Rane asks.

I think about the circle. The bare wrist. Trey's eyes. Silas's smile.

"I survived," I say.

It's not an answer. They know it's not an answer.

But no one pushes.

We walk home together, and I don't look back.

# Chapter 14
## TREY

I don't know what just happened.

I'm walking beside Silas, same as always, but my head is still back in that room. Back in the hallway. Back with her.

Nova.

She looked at me like—I don't know. Like she recognized something. Like my words meant something to her that I didn't even know they meant.

*I couldn't figure out who I wanted to be.*

I said it without thinking. Looked right at her when I said it. And she didn't look away.

"So that's her," Silas says.

His voice pulls me back. We're outside now, cutting across the quad toward the east buildings. The afternoon light is too bright after that small room.

"What?"

"The anomaly. The one who showed up out of nowhere." He says it casually, like he's talking about the weather. "No mark. That's interesting."

I don't like the way he says *interesting*.

"She's part of that cluster," I say. "The one that formed before the system caught it."

"I know." Silas glances at me. "Harrick's been doing some digging. Apparently she was off-grid for fifteen years. No trace, no contact, nothing. And then suddenly she just... shows up. Already attached to *them*."

The way he says *them* tells me everything.

"So?"

"So doesn't that seem convenient to you?" He's not looking at me now, eyes scanning the quad like he's bored. But I know better. "Fifteen years outside the system. No mark. And she lands in the middle of the one cluster no one knows what to do with. Five guys from five different Houses who somehow found each other before the system had no choice but to recognize it." He shakes his head. "They're a mess. An embarrassment. And now they've got a sixth who's even more broken than they are."

"What are you saying?"

"I'm not saying anything." He shrugs. "Just that it's a lot of coincidences. And I don't believe in coincidences."

We walk in silence for a few steps. I should let it drop. I should change the subject, talk about training or schedules or anything else.

"What did you think of her?" I ask instead.

Silas's mouth curves. Not quite a smile. "I think she's scared. I think she doesn't belong here. And I think that blank wrist is going to cause problems."

"Problems for who?"

"Everyone." He looks at me sideways. "Why? What did you think of her?"

I think about gray joggers and silver-blonde hair and pale blue eyes that held mine across a circle. I think about the way her hands shook when she extended her wrist. The way she started to stand, started to run, and then sat back down because the professor told her to.

I think about the hallway. The way she stopped when I called her name even though she didn't have to.

"I don't know yet," I say.

It's not a lie. But it's not the truth either.

Silas watches me for a second too long. Then he nods, like I just confirmed something.

"Be careful, Trey."

"Of what?"

"Of getting curious about things that aren't good for you."

I know a threat when I hear one.

"She's in my class," I say. "That's all."

"You should probably keep it that way."

I'm done talking. We've reached the training building anyway, and Silas pulls open the door without waiting for me.

I follow him inside, but my mind is still on the quad. Still on the circle. Still on her.

*I couldn't figure out who I wanted to be.*

She looked at me like she understood.

I should probably worry about that.

At least I know I'm going to see her again. Mark Theory meets twice a week.

Twice a week, sitting across from her in that circle. Twice a week, watching Silas watch her.

I don't like it.

I don't like any of it.

But I can't stop thinking about the way she looked at me, and that's a problem I don't have a solution for yet.

# Chapter 15
## RANE

I can't get this girl out of my head.

It's been a week. Okay, a week and a half. And I've literally rearranged my entire life around her. We all have. Schedules shifted, routines rewritten, every decision filtered through where is she and is she okay and does she need something.

It's terrifying. It's stupid.

I love it.

She's eating more now. Not a lot, but more. Between the five of us, we've figured out how to get food in front of her without making it a thing. Vaelor leaves plates where she'll find them. Beckett keeps the fridge stocked with stuff she likes. Kyron "accidentally" orders too much when we get takeout. Locke doesn't say anything, but he's started making sure there's always bread on the table because he noticed she reaches for it first.

And me? I just talk. Fill the silence so she doesn't have to think about what she's putting in her mouth, just does it while she's distracted.

It's working. Even in the short time she's been here, she looks better. Healthier. The shadows under her eyes aren't as deep. Her cheeks have a little more color. She doesn't flinch as hard when one of us moves too fast.

And she's fucking beautiful.

I said it before, and I'll keep saying it until she believes it. I just might not say it out loud again for a while yet.

Now if we could just keep Harrick and his lackeys away from her.

They've been circling. Nothing direct—not since that first morning on the path. But I see them watching. Silas especially. He's in her Mark Theory class, and every time she comes back from it, she's wound tight in a way that takes hours to fade.

We can't be in that room with her. It's the one place she's unprotected.

I fucking hate it.

But today's Sunday. No classes. No Harrick. Just the house and the five of us and her, and I'm going to focus on that instead of all the ways this could go wrong.

The phone arrives after breakfast.

I'm the one who ordered it. Set it up myself—our numbers saved, everything configured so she just has to turn it on. The guys gave me shit about it, but someone had to do it, and I wanted to be the one.

I wanted to be the one to give her something.

I find her in her room.

The door's open a few inches, and I knock on the frame before pushing it wider. She's sitting on her bed, legs crossed, a book open in her lap that she's clearly not reading. When she looks up, something in my chest does a stupid little flip.

"Hey," I say. "Got something for you."

I hold up the phone. Her eyebrows pull together.

"You didn't have to—"

"Yeah, I did. We need to be able to reach you." I cross the room before she can argue and sit down on the bed beside her. "Here. It's already set up. All our numbers are in there."

She takes it carefully, like it might bite her. Turns it over in her hands.

"I don't really know how to..."

"I'll show you."

I shift closer. Lean in so I can see the screen, my arm coming up behind her. Not touching, but close. Close enough that I can smell her shampoo—something soft, a little floral. Close enough that I can feel the warmth of her.

"Okay, so this is the home screen," I say, and my voice comes out mostly normal. "You swipe up to unlock. Contacts are here—see? That's all of us. You tap a name to call, or you can text by—"

She leans into me.

Not a lot. Just a fraction. Like her body decided to do it without asking her brain first. Her shoulder presses against my chest and she makes this tiny sound—barely a breath, almost a sigh—and I forget what I was saying.

I forget everything.

"Rane?"

My name in her mouth. She's turned her head to look at me and her face is right there, inches away, and her eyes drop to my mouth for just a second before snapping back up.

Oh fuck.

"Yeah?" My voice is not normal. My voice is wrecked and I haven't even done anything.

"You stopped talking."

"Did I?"

"You were showing me the contacts."

"Right. Yeah. Contacts."

I need to move. I need to put space between us before I do something stupid. But she's still leaning into me and her eyes are still on my face and I can see the pulse jumping in her throat and—

I stand up so fast I almost knock her over.

"That's—you've got it. You're good. The guys are all in there, so if you need anything, just—yeah."

Smooth, Rane. Really smooth.

She blinks up at me, confusion flickering across her face. "Are you okay?"

"Great. I'm great. Just remembered I have to—there's a thing. Downstairs. I should go do the thing."

I'm already backing toward the door. My heel catches on something—might be my own stupid feet—and I stumble, catching myself on the doorframe.

Her lips twitch. Just a little.

"Thanks for the phone," she says.

"Yep. Welcome. Enjoy."

I escape into the hallway and pull the door mostly shut behind me, then stand there for a second with my hand on the wall, trying to remember how to breathe.

*What the fuck was that?*

Her shoulder against my chest. That little sound she made. The way she looked at my mouth.

I need to walk this off. I need to think about something else. I need to—

I make it to the common room and Kyron is on the couch, phone in hand, and he looks up when I come in.

His eyebrows rise.

"You okay there?"

"Fine," I say. Too fast.

"You look like you just ran a marathon."

"I didn't."

"Your face is red."

"It's not."

"It is." He sets the phone down. Those blue eyes are way too sharp. "What happened?"

"Nothing."

"Rane."

"I was showing her the phone."

"And?"

I run a hand through my hair. Pace toward the window. Turn back.

"She leaned into me."

Kyron goes very still.

"And she made this—this sound. And then she looked at my mouth, Kyron. She looked at my mouth."

Silence.

"So what did you do?" he asks.

"I left."

"You left."

"I excused myself."

"Smoothly?"

I think about tripping over her shoe. About saying *there's a thing* like an absolute idiot.

"Not exactly."

Kyron's mouth twitches. Then he's laughing—not loud, but real—and I want to be annoyed but I can't because he's right. I'm a disaster.

"It's not funny," I say, but I'm almost smiling now too.

"It's a little funny." He shakes his head. "You've got it bad."

"Shut up."

"We all do. You're just the worst at hiding it."

I drop onto the other end of the couch and stare at the ceiling.

He's not wrong.

I've got it so bad, and she looked at my mouth, and now all I can think about is what she tastes like.

# Chapter 16
## Nova

I'm still sitting on the bed, phone in my hand, staring at the door Rane just stumbled through.

What the fuck was that?

I can still feel where his chest pressed against my shoulder. Still smell whatever soap he uses—something warm, a little spicy. Still hear the way his voice went rough when he said my name.

And I looked at his mouth. I looked at his lips like—

No. Stop. That was nothing. He was just close. People get close sometimes. It doesn't mean anything.

Except my heart is still pounding and I can still smell him and I kind of want him to come back.

Fuck.

This isn't just about being close.

It felt like... I don't know, like I wanted to kiss him. Like I wanted to get closer.

I think.

I'm honestly not sure what that feels like.

I shove that thought down so hard it should leave a bruise.

The phone is still warm in my hand. I look at the screen, swipe up like Rane showed me. The contacts are right there. Five names. Five numbers. Five people who rearranged their schedules so I wouldn't be alone on my first day. Who feed me without making it weird. Who are always just... there.

I don't know what to do with that. I don't know what to do with any of this.

A knock at the door.

I shove the phone under my pillow like I was doing something wrong, which is stupid because I wasn't, and say, "Yeah?"

The door opens and Beckett's standing there. He looks—different. There's something in his expression I haven't seen before. Almost like he's trying not to smile.

"Someone's here for you," he says.

"What?"

"Downstairs."

He doesn't explain. Just steps back and waits for me to follow.

I get up, suddenly aware that I'm still in the same joggers I slept in, hair probably a disaster. But Beckett's already heading down the hall, so I grab the phone and follow.

The living room is full and everyone's acting like they have a secret.

All five of them, trying way too hard to look casual. Rane won't look at me at all, which makes my face warm for reasons I'm not examining.

Someone clears their throat.

And in the middle of all of them, grinning like she's won the lottery, is Zoe.

"There she is!" Zoe crosses the room and grabs my hands before I can react. "I'm stealing you."

"Stealing me?"

"Shopping. Lunch. Girl time." She tugs me toward the door. "You've been drowning in testosterone for almost two weeks. You need a break."

I look back at the guys. They're all doing a very bad job of acting normal. Kyron's on the couch with his phone but he keeps glancing up. Vaelor looks like he's very interested in the floor. Rane's watching me with something soft in his expression that makes my stomach flip.

"Have fun," Locke says. Almost warm. For him.

Weird.

Zoe laughs and pulls me out the door before I can figure out what's going on.

The shopping center is bright and loud and overwhelming in a completely different way than the Academy. Places like this used to watch me through the window until I moved on. Security would appear if I lingered too long near an entrance. Shop owners would find reasons to step outside, arms crossed, waiting for me to take the hint.

Now Zoe pulls me through the doors like I belong here. Holds up clothes against me, asks my opinion, actually listens when I say what I like. No one asks us to leave. No one watches to make sure I don't steal anything.

It's disorienting. I keep waiting for someone to notice I'm not supposed to be here.

It's... nice. Weird, but nice.

"Okay, this," she says, shoving a soft forest green sweater into my arms. "This is perfect for you. Try it on."

"I don't need—"

"Try it on."

I try it on. It fits. It's the softest thing I've ever worn.

"We're getting it," Zoe says, and before I can argue she's already taken it to the register.

"Zoe, I can't—I don't have any money."

"Don't worry about it."

"I'm not letting you pay for—"

"I'm not paying for it." She pulls a card out of her wallet and hands it to the cashier. The name on it reads KYRON VALE.

I stare at it.

"What is that?"

Zoe winces. "Shit."

"Zoe."

"I wasn't supposed to—look, it's fine, they wanted—"

"Tell me."

She sighs, handing the bag to me and steering me away from the register. "Come on. I know just the place for this conversation."

She leads me to a beauty counter in the center of the floor. A woman in a sleek black uniform looks up as we approach.

"Can I help you ladies?"

"She needs everything," Zoe says, depositing me onto the stool like I'm a package. "Full face. Make her glow."

"Zoe—"

"You'll love it. Trust me." She hops onto the stool next to mine, getting comfortable. "And while she works, we talk."

The woman—her nametag says MIRA—tilts my chin up, studying my face. "You have gorgeous bone structure. Those cheekbones." She starts pulling out products. "Special occasion?"

"She just joined a cluster," Zoe says.

Mira's hands still for just a second. When she looks at me again, there's something new in her expression. "Oh. Congratulations."

"Thanks," I manage, not sure what I'm being congratulated for.

"Five guys," Zoe adds. "All absurdly good-looking. It's disgusting, honestly."

Mira laughs, but there's an edge of wistfulness to it. "Five? God." She shakes her head, dabbing primer onto my skin. "You're a lucky girl."

I blink. "I am?"

"Most of us spend our whole lives hoping for a bond. Any bond. And clusters?" She whistles low. "That's the dream. The real thing."

I catch Zoe's eye. She's watching me carefully.

"Okay, so," Zoe says. "The guys asked me to do this."

"Do what, exactly?"

"Take you shopping. Get you things you need. Stuff you actually want, not just whatever was in that dresser." She pulls out another card—this one reads LOCKE MERCER—and holds it up. "They gave me backups. Plural. And very specific instructions to make sure you didn't argue about it."

Mira pauses with a brush halfway to my face. "They gave her their cards?"

"Multiple."

"And they're not even bonded yet?"

"Nope."

Mira stares at me like I've grown a second head. "Honey. Do you understand what that means?"

I don't. I really don't.

"It means they're already gone for you," Mira says, returning to my face with renewed focus. "Men don't do that. Not unless they're sure."

"Sure of what?"

She and Zoe exchange a look I can't read.

"Close your eyes," Mira says. "I'm doing your lids."

I close them. The brush moves soft across my eyelids.

"When I first met my guys," Zoe says slowly, "I thought I was losing my mind. Everything felt too much. Too fast. I couldn't be in a room with them without my skin feeling like it was on fire. I didn't understand why I kept wanting to be near them even when it scared me."

My chest tightens. That's—that's exactly—

"What does that mean?" I ask. My voice comes out smaller than I want it to.

"You'll see," Zoe says.

"That's not an answer."

"I know."

Mira finishes my eyes and moves to my lips. "She's right, though. It doesn't make sense until it does. And then it's the only thing that's ever made sense."

"You're in a cluster too?" I ask.

"Bonded six years ago. Three men." She smiles, soft and private. "Best thing that ever happened to me."

She finishes and steps back, turning my stool toward the mirror.

I don't recognize myself.

The face looking back at me has color, definition, *life*. Cheekbones I didn't know I had. Eyes that look bigger, brighter. Lips that look soft and full.

I look like someone who matters.

"Oh," Mira says quietly. "Oh, you're going to destroy them."

We leave with a bag full of products Mira insisted I needed—skincare, mascara, lip gloss, a little palette of eyeshadows she swore was foolproof. A perfume she spritzed on my wrist, something soft and warm with a hint of vanilla. Things I've watched other women use my whole life and never thought I'd own.

We hit two more stores. Pajamas that aren't scratchy. Basics that actually fit.

And then Zoe stops dead in front of a window display.

"Oh," she says. "Oh, no. We're going in."

"Zoe—"

She's already pulling me through the door.

The store is all leather and lace and things I would never look at twice. Zoe moves through it like she has a target locked, and before I can protest she's shoving something white into my hands.

"Try this on."

I look down. White leather pants. A top that's half corset, half sleeve—white lace over skin on one side, fitted white leather on the other. A silver chain choker.

"I can't wear this."

"Why not?"

"Because I—" I don't have an answer. Because it's too much. Because it's not me. Because I've spent fifteen years wearing things that help me disappear and this is the opposite of disappearing.

"Just try it," Zoe says. Softer now. "For fun. You don't have to buy it."

I go into the dressing room because it's easier than arguing.

The leather slides on like it was made for me. The lace sits against my skin, delicate and strange. The chain settles at my throat, cool and light.

I look in the mirror.

I don't recognize myself.

Not in a bad way. In a way that makes my breath catch. The white against my pale hair, my pale skin—I look like something out of a dream. Or a nightmare. I can't decide which.

"Nova?" Zoe's voice through the door. "You okay in there?"

I open it.

Zoe's eyes go wide. "Holy shit."

"It's too much."

"It's *perfect*." She grabs my shoulders and turns me toward the mirror outside the dressing room. "Look at yourself. Actually look."

I look.

The girl in the mirror doesn't look like someone who sleeps in alleys. She doesn't look like someone who learned to be invisible. She looks like someone who could walk into a room and make people stop talking.

She looks like someone who belongs somewhere.

"We're getting it," Zoe says.

"I don't need—"

"This isn't about need." She's already pulling out Kyron's card. "This is about want. When's the last time you let yourself want something?"

I... I don't know.

We're halfway back to the house, bags in hand, when I finally ask.

"Zoe?"

"Yeah?"

"The thing you said. About your guys. About your skin feeling like it was on fire."

She glances at me sideways. "Yeah?"

"Does it ever stop?"

She laughs—not mean, just surprised. "No. It just starts making sense."

I don't know what that means. But I'm still thinking about it when we get back—the fire under the skin, the wanting to be near them even when it's terrifying.

That's exactly how I feel.

And I have no idea what to do with it.

# Chapter 17
## LOCKE

I'm sitting on the front steps for no reason.

That's the lie I'm telling myself. The truth is I've been out here for twenty minutes watching the path like she's going to appear on it. Like the impatient stalker I am who knows she's gonna be done shopping soon only because the stores are about to close and I want to be the first one she sees.

The others are inside. I told them I needed air.

No one believed me. No one said anything either.

I see them before I hear them. Two figures coming up the path—Zoe's dark hair, easy stride. And next to her—

My chest locks.

Nova.

Something soft. Warm. Vanilla layered over something else, something I've already memorized without meaning to. Her. It cuts through the evening air like it's the only thing that exists.

I breathe in again. Deeper. Testing.

Still there. Still *her*.

She's too far away to smell. That's the thing. She's at least thirty feet out, maybe more, and there's no wind, and I shouldn't be able to—

But I can.

Mine.

The word hits before I can stop it.

There's no logic or reason. Just truth, declared by something deeper than my brain. Something that doesn't give a fuck about what's possible.

My hands curl into fists on my knees. Something in my chest is pulling, tightening, like a rope being wound around a drum. I can feel my pulse in my throat, in my temples, behind my eyes.

*Mine.*

She's closer now. Carrying bags, hair down, catching the late afternoon light, and—

I forget what I was thinking.

Something's different. Her face. Her *mouth*. Soft pink and I can't stop looking at it, can't make myself look anywhere else, and she's wearing the same clothes she left in but she doesn't look the same. She looks like someone finally showed her what I've been seeing this whole time.

I can't breathe.

Zoe sees me first.

Her stride doesn't falter but something shifts in her face—a knowing look that turns into a smirk. Her eyes move from my face to my fists to my face again, and I watch her decide not to say anything.

Smart.

They stop at the bottom of the steps. Zoe leans in close to Nova, says something I can't hear. Nova's brow furrows, confused. Then Zoe's stepping back, already turning toward her own place.

She catches my eye as she goes. Mouths *breathe* at me like I'm a disaster she's enjoying.

Then she's gone, and Nova is standing at the bottom of the steps looking up at me, and every single thought in my head whites out.

She's close now. Close enough that the scent isn't a question anymore—it's an assault. Vanilla and warmth and *her*, flooding my lungs, soaking into my bloodstream. I can feel it in my teeth. In my fucking *bones*.

"Hey," she says.

Her voice is uncertain. Her shoulders are creeping up toward her ears. She's watching my face, trying to read it, and I realize I must look—

I don't know what I look like. I don't know what's showing. But whatever it is, it's making her shrink.

"Is everything okay?" she asks. "You look—"

She stops. Swallows.

"Sorry." She's already turning away, already retreating. "I'm probably reading this wrong. I'll just—"

No.

*No.*

"Nova."

Her name comes out wrecked. Scraped raw. She freezes mid-turn.

I'm on my feet. I don't remember standing. I'm down one step, then another, and she's watching me come toward her like she can't decide if she should run.

Good instincts. She should run.

I stop close enough to touch. Close enough to see her pupils blow wide, her lips part, the quick rise of her chest as her breathing goes shallow.

"You're not reading it wrong," I say. My voice doesn't sound like mine. "You're the most beautiful thing I've ever seen."

She looks like she wants to say something but no sound comes out.

I should stop. I should give her space, let her process, be the steady one. That's who I am. That's who I've always been.

But my hand is already moving.

I watch it like it belongs to someone else—rising, reaching, brushing her jaw with my knuckles. Her skin is so soft it makes my chest ache. Her eyes flutter closed and something inside me *snaps*.

*Mine. Take her. Claim her. Make her understand she's yours.*

The thoughts come from somewhere deep and dark, somewhere I didn't know existed. It's a demand I can't afford right now. Because that's not what she deserves. My blood is running hot, too hot, and there's a pressure building at the base of my skull that feels like—

I don't know what, but whatever it is wants *out*.

I lean in.

*Slow. Gentle. Don't scare her.*

I'm bargaining with myself. Negotiating with whatever is clawing at the inside of my ribs, trying to get out.

*Just a taste. Just one. Then stop.*

My lips brush hers.

The world ends.

She's soft. So fucking soft. She tastes like lip gloss and something sweeter underneath, something that's just *her*, and I want to drown in it. I want to consume her. I want to pin her against the railing and kiss her until she can't remember anyone's name but mine.

I don't.

I keep it gentle. Soft. A question instead of a demand.

It's the hardest thing I've ever done.

She kisses me back—tentative, uncertain, like she's not quite sure what to do. Like she's following my lead because she doesn't...

*This is her first kiss.*

The realization hits me like a punch to the gut. Her *first*. I'm her first. No one else has ever—

A sound escapes my throat. Something between a groan and a growl. My hand slides from her jaw into her hair, cupping the back of her head, and I have to physically stop myself from deepening the kiss. From taking more. From showing her exactly what I want to do to her.

*Gentle. She's not ready. She doesn't know.*

I'm shaking. Actually shaking. Every muscle in my body is locked tight, fighting the thing inside me that wants to devour her whole.

I pull back.

It takes everything I have.

Her eyes open slowly. Dazed. Her cheeks are flushed and her lips are swollen and she's looking at me like I just rearranged the entire universe without warning her first.

The bags are on the ground. I don't know when she dropped them.

My hand is still in her hair. I should let go. I know I should. But she hasn't pulled away, hasn't stiffened, hasn't given me any sign that she wants me to stop touching her.

So I don't.

"Locke," she whispers.

I'm never getting that taste out of my mouth. I'm never going to stop wanting more. I'm going to spend the rest of my life chasing this exact moment, this exact feeling, this exact—

The door opens behind me.

We both freeze.

Kyron stands in the doorway. His eyes move from me to Nova to the dropped bags to her swollen lips. His expression doesn't change, but something in his posture goes very still.

Nova bolts.

She grabs the bags—misses one, grabs it again—and pushes past Kyron into the house without a word. Her footsteps pound up the stairs. A door slams.

Silence.

Kyron steps out onto the porch. The door clicks shut behind him.

"Well," he says. His voice is too casual. "You lucky son of a bitch."

I don't say anything. I'm still staring at the spot where she was standing.

"I really didn't think you'd be the first." He moves to stand beside me, arms crossed, looking out at the path like this is a normal conversation. "How was it?"

The question lands somewhere in my chest and twists.

"Better," I say.

Kyron is quiet for a long moment.

"Better than what?"

"Better than anything I've ever imagined."

He exhales. Slow. Controlled. When I glance at him, his jaw is tight.

"She ran," he says.

I know. I felt it. The moment the door opened, she was gone—like a rabbit spooked by a predator.

"She'll run from all of us," I say. "At first."

"And then?"

I look at him. "And then she won't."

Kyron holds my gaze. We've known this was coming. All of us wanting the same person, all of us having to figure out how to make that work. It's not a problem yet. It will be.

"Next time," he says, "at least warn a guy."

Then he goes back inside.

I stay on the steps.

The sun is starting to set. The air is cooling. I can still taste her on my lips, still smell her perfume.

I was calm once.

I remember it.

Before she walked up those steps like she already belonged to me.

# Chapter 18
## NOVA

I don't go down for dinner.

I hear them. Voices through the floor, the clatter of plates, someone laughing at something. Normal sounds. The sounds of people who didn't just ruin everything by kissing one of their housemates on the front steps like an idiot.

I sit on the edge of my bed and stare at the wall.

*I kissed him.*

No. He kissed me. He moved first. His hand on my jaw, his mouth on mine, and I just—

I kissed him back.

My face burns. I press my palms against my cheeks like I can push the heat back in.

*What is wrong with me?*

They let me stay here. They gave me a room and food and walked me to class and didn't ask for anything. And I repaid that by—

I can't even finish the thought.

The smell of dinner drifts up through the floor. My stomach cramps but I don't move. I'm not going down there. I'm not sitting at that table with all of them while Locke looks at me and they all *know*.

Do they know?

Kyron saw. He was standing right there. He saw my face, my lips, the bags on the ground. He knows.

Which means they all know by now.

I pull my knees up to my chest and wrap my arms around them.

*I ruined it.*

The thought settles in my chest like a stone. I had something. For two weeks I had something—a place to sleep, people who showed up, a version of normal I'd never had before. And now it's going to get weird. They're going to pull back. Start treating me differently. Start exchanging looks when they think I'm not watching.

I've seen it before. Not this, not exactly, but close enough. The way people shift when you become a problem. The way the air changes right before they decide you're not worth the trouble.

I should have known better.

I should have *been* better.

The house goes quiet eventually. Footsteps on the stairs, doors closing, the creak of the old floors settling. I don't move. I sit in the dark with my arms around my knees and I don't sleep.

The phone sits on my nightstand. I haven't touched it.

I grab it before I can talk myself out of it. Unlock the screen.

One text.

**Beckett:** *You okay?*

Two words. Sent at 11:47pm. Six hours ago. He waited up.

I lock the phone and put it face down on the nightstand.

I don't know how to answer that. I don't know how to answer anything right now.

His hand in my hair. The sound he made against my mouth. The way he looked at me after, like I'd done something to him he wasn't expecting.

*I didn't mean to.*

But that's not true either. I could have stepped back. I could have turned my head. I could have done anything except stand there and let him kiss me and then kiss him back like I'd been waiting for it.

*Had* I been waiting for it?

No. No. That's not—

I think about Zoe. The bench at the makeup counter. The way she looked at me when she said *you'll see.*

*"I couldn't be in a room with them without my skin feeling like it was on fire. I didn't understand why I kept wanting to be near them even when it scared me."*

I told her that wasn't me. That I didn't feel that way.

I'm such a liar.

But it doesn't matter what I want. It matters what I *did*. And what I did was kiss someone I'm living with and then run away like a scared animal.

Great. Really great start.

I get dressed in the dark. Grab my bag. Check the time.

Early. Way too early. But I can't stay in this room and I can't go downstairs and sit at that table and pretend everything's normal.

So I leave.

The hallway is quiet. The house is still. I make it to the top of the stairs and start down, keeping my footsteps light, keeping my breathing even, keeping my eyes on the door like if I just get through it everything will be fine.

Beckett is leaning against the wall by the entrance.

I see him. Pale pink hair, dark eyes, tattoos disappearing under his sleeves. He's holding a mug of something, steam curling up, and he's watching me come down the stairs with an expression I can't read.

I don't stop.

I don't say good morning or hi or sorry or any of the things a normal person would say. I just adjust my grip on my bag and walk past him and push through the door and I'm outside, I'm out, I'm gone.

The air is cold. Good. Fine. I can work with cold.

I walk.

The campus is mostly empty this early. A few people heading to the gym, a maintenance cart humming down a side path. I don't look at any of them. I just walk, fast, like I'm late for something, like there's somewhere I need to be that isn't just *away*.

My thoughts won't stop.

*What if it changes everything?*

It already has. It changed the second his mouth touched mine.

*What if they act weird?*

They will. Of course they will. Kyron already looked at me different. The others will too. They won't say anything—they'll just stop meeting my eyes. Start closing doors when I walk into the room.

I walk faster.

*What if they pretend it didn't happen?*

That might be worse. Sitting across from Locke at breakfast while everyone acts like I didn't have my fingers in his shirt and his hand in my hair and—

*What if they don't care?*

My chest tightens. That's the worst option. The one where it meant nothing. Where I've been awake all night over something he's already forgotten.

I've seen this before. I know what it looks like when people decide you're too much.

*It didn't mean anything.*

I try the thought on. It doesn't fit.

*It was adrenaline. The shopping trip. The makeover. I was overwhelmed and he was there and it just happened.*

Closer. But still wrong.

*I didn't even mean to. He moved first.*

True. But I didn't pull away.

I didn't *want* to pull away.

And that's what I keep circling back to. Not what he did. What I did. What I wanted.

What I'm still wanting.

*Fuck.*

*They were kind to me. I ruined it.*

The thought settles into my chest like something with teeth.

*You finally had something real. A place. People. And you couldn't just—*

I don't finish the thought. I don't have to. I already know how this ends. I've lived it enough times to recognize it.

It's better if... I can't finish the thought.

The path curves. I'm not paying attention to where I'm going. My feet know the route to the main building and they're taking it without consulting me.

*Just get through today. One class. Then figure out the rest.*

I round a corner.

I don't see him until it's too late.

I walk directly into a chest. A very large, very solid chest that doesn't move when I hit it.

"Shit," I breathe.

Then I look up.

And everything gets worse.

# Chapter 19
## BECKETT

She doesn't look back.

That's how I know.

I'm standing by the door with my coffee going cold, watching her cross the threshold like she's late for something. Bag over her shoulder, head down, moving fast. She saw me. I know she did. But she didn't stop, didn't say morning, didn't do any of the things a person does when they're planning to come back.

She just left.

And something in the way she moved—the set of her shoulders, the angle of her chin, the way she didn't even hesitate at the door—

I've seen flight before. That wasn't retreat. That was escape.

I set the mug down. My hands are steady but my chest isn't.

Locke told us last night. All of it. The kiss, the way she froze, the way she grabbed her bags and bolted the second Kyron opened the door. He told us because that's what we agreed—no secrets, not about her, not about this. We're too close to the edge for anything less than full transparency.

But she doesn't know that. She doesn't know we talked about it, doesn't know we've been waiting for her to come downstairs, doesn't know we spent half the night figuring out how to make this easier for her.

She doesn't know any of it.

Because no one's seen her since. Not a word, not a text, not even footsteps in the hallway. Silence, and now this.

I take the stairs two at a time.

Rane's door is first. I don't knock. Just shove it open, hit the lights.

"Get up."

He's blinking at me, half-asleep, confused. "What—"

"Everyone. Kitchen. Now."

I don't wait for a response. Kyron's door next, then Vaelor's. Locke's already opening his by the time I get there, reading something in my face that makes his jaw go tight.

"What happened?"

"Kitchen."

Five minutes later we're all there. Vaelor's at the counter, hands moving on autopilot—coffee, mugs, the familiar rhythm of morning. But his eyes keep flicking to me. They all keep flicking to me.

Because I don't do this. I don't slam doors and yell and drag everyone out of bed. That's not who I am.

Which means they know something's wrong.

"She's gone," I say.

Silence.

Kyron sets down his phone. "What?"

"What the hell do you mean she's gone?" Rane's voice pitches up.

"She's here." Locke's already moving toward the stairs. "She's sleeping. She's—"

"No." I step into his path. "I watched her walk out the door less than ten minutes ago."

He stops. Stares at me.

"Why didn't you fucking stop her?"

"It's not my place."

"The hell it isn't."

"Locke." Vaelor's voice cuts through, low and steady. "Calm down."

"Don't tell me to calm down." But he stops moving. His hands are fists at his sides, knuckles white. "She's out there alone and he just watched her leave."

"She might be ours." The word scrapes coming out, but I say it anyway. "But she's still her own person. I can't force her to stay. None of us can."

"So what, we just let her go?"

"I didn't say that."

The kitchen goes quiet. Vaelor's stopped pretending to make coffee. Rane's got one hand pressed flat against the counter like he needs it to stay upright. Kyron's watching me with that sharp, assessing look he gets when he's running calculations I can't see.

"I couldn't be sure," I say. Slower now. "Can't be. But my gut says she's not coming back."

Vaelor meets my eyes. "Your gut's not usually wrong, is it?"

"No. It's not."

More silence. The kind that presses down.

Rane breaks first. "So what do we do? Are we just going to sit here talking about it?"

"We need to get her back." Locke's voice is rough. "Obviously we need to get her back."

"Of course we do." I look at Locke. He's the one most likely to blow past me and out the door. "But we need to do it right."

"Is there a right way here?" Rane asks.

"Yes."

They wait.

"Because if we don't do this right," I say, "we may lose her before we ever had her in the first place."

No one argues.

No one has anything to say to that.

# Chapter 20
## NOVA

I step back fast, heart slamming.

"S-sorry."

But I already know. I knew the second I hit him. The size, the stillness, the way the air went wrong.

Silas looks down at me. He's not smiling, but something in his face is worse than a smile.

Harrick steps out from behind him, grinning. "Well look who it is."

*Fuck. Fuck fuck fuck.*

"I was just—" I start.

"Just what?" Harrick tilts his head. "Out for a little morning rejection walk? If you're not getting what you need from those idiots, we can help you out."

My skin crawls. "No, I was just on my way to—"

"This early?" Silas's voice is quieter than Harrick's. Colder. "I don't think so."

I take another step back. My heel catches on a crack in the path and I have to catch myself.

Harrick's grin widens. "So let's see it. The mark." He pauses, savoring it. "Or, you know. The part where it should be."

"No."

I'm already backing up but he's faster. His hand closes around my wrist and yanks my sleeve up before I can pull away. I try to twist free but his grip tightens, holding me in place.

Silas moves closer.

He doesn't grab me. He doesn't have to. He just reaches out, slow and deliberate, and runs one finger along the inside of my wrist.

My stomach lurches. His touch makes my skin crawl.

Silas is watching my face. My gut tells me to run.

He doesn't act on whatever he sees. But he doesn't step back either.

"I thought it was a trick," he says. Still touching my wrist. Still watching my face. "I mean, come on. No mark? That doesn't happen."

Harrick laughs. "How are you even here?"

I try to pull my arm back. Harrick holds it.

"No wonder your little cluster doesn't want you," he says. "What do you even have to offer them?"

"Let go of me."

"Fifteen years on the street." He's not letting go. "Sleeping in trash. Eating out of the garbage. And they're supposed to believe you belong with them?"

My throat closes. "How do you—"

"Doesn't matter." Silas nods at Harrick, who drops my wrist. But Silas's eyes don't leave my face. "What matters is you were exactly where you belonged. Invisible. And the only reason you're here now is because the system made a mistake."

I can feel the tears starting. I hate it. I hate that they can see it, hate that I'm giving them this, hate that everything they're saying is exactly what I've been telling myself since I got here.

"You don't belong here," Harrick says. "You know that, right? You're not one of them. You're not one of anyone."

Silas is still watching me. Still calculating. Like he's figuring out what I am. Like he wants to crack me open and see what's inside.

"Maybe you should go back to where you came from," he says. Soft. Almost gentle. "Before someone gets hurt."

They're both smiling now.

I run.

I don't know where I'm going. The path blurs, my breath too loud in my ears, and I don't care. I just need to move. I need to get away from their laughter, from Silas's eyes, from the sound of my own history being thrown back at me like proof of everything I already knew.

I don't belong here.

I never did.

The campus gates are ahead. I don't slow down.

I have to get out.

# Chapter 21
## Trey

I round the corner just in time to see her disappear.

Silver-blonde hair, moving fast. Gone before I can call out, before I can even be sure it was her. But I know. Something in my chest knows.

Harrick and Silas are standing in the middle of the path, watching the spot where she vanished. Harrick's laughing. Silas looks like he just scraped something off his shoe.

"Was that—"

"Does it matter?" Harrick cuts me off.

Silas's expression flattens. "You know exactly who it was."

I look at where she disappeared. Back at them.

"Nova."

"Of course." Harrick grins. "The little misfit finally figured out where she belongs."

My hands curl into fists.

"You didn't."

Silas raises an eyebrow. Doesn't answer.

"Tell me you fucking didn't."

Harrick laughs, loud and easy like this is all a joke. "Chill out, man. What's it to you?"

Silas tilts his head. Studies me. "Oh, that's right. She's your little girlfriend now, isn't she? Did you forget to mention that to us?"

Harrick howls. "Holy shit. This is a joke, right? You can't be serious."

"Enough."

The word comes out harder than I mean it to. Harrick's laughter dies. Silas just watches me, that same flat expression, like he's waiting to see what I'll do.

"What, Trey?" His voice is soft. Almost amused. "You can dish it out but you can't take it?"

"That's not—"

"What are you going to do? Huff and puff?" He steps closer. "You've been right here with us plenty of times. Don't pretend you're better than this."

My jaw tightens. He's not wrong. I've stood next to them. Laughed at the same shit. Looked the other way when I should have looked closer.

But this is different.

"Don't fucking tempt me."

Harrick snorts. "You don't have the balls anyway."

I'm done.

"Where the hell did she go?"

Harrick shrugs. "Who knows? Who cares? She's fucking gone. That's all that matters."

"No."

Silence. Silas's eyes narrow.

"If you're so concerned," he says slowly, "go after her."

He lets that sit. Then:

"But if you do, you can kiss that internship with my father goodbye. You know the one. The one that's going to set you up after graduation." He smiles. "You really want to throw that away for some broken girl who doesn't even have a mark?"

I stare at him.

Two years. Two years of swallowing shit I didn't agree with because I needed what his family could offer. Two years of telling myself it was temporary, that I'd get out eventually, that the ends justified the means.

Two years of being exactly the kind of person who'd let Nova run off alone after they made her cry.

"You know what?"

Silas waits.

"Tell your father to go fuck himself."

Harrick's mouth drops open.

"Stay the fuck away from her. Both of you."

Harrick scoffs. "And if we don't?"

"Then the scholarship won't be the only thing I'm willing to lose."

I turn and walk. Then run.

I don't know where she went. I don't know if I can find her. I don't know what I'm going to say if I do.

But I'm not letting her stay gone.

# Chapter 22
## VAELOR

I've checked the library twice. The dining hall. The back paths behind the training buildings where no one goes this early.

Nothing.

She's not here. Or if she is, she doesn't want to be found—and Nova knows how to not be found. Fifteen years of practice. Years of learning how to disappear when disappearing was the only thing keeping her alive.

I keep moving. I can't stop.

If I stop, I'll think too much, and if I think too much I'll remember her face at dinner two nights ago—the way she reached for the bread like she was still surprised it was there, the way she almost smiled when Rane said something stupid, the way she looked at all of us like she was waiting for the catch.

There's no catch. That's what I wanted to tell her. There's no catch, there's no trick, there's just us, and we're not going anywhere.

But I didn't say it. None of us did. And now she's gone.

I cut through the east quad toward the meeting point. We agreed to regroup every twenty minutes, share what we've got, adjust the search grid. It's inefficient but it's better than five of us running in circles while she slips further away.

The morning air is cold. I didn't grab a jacket. Didn't think about it. Just moved.

My chest is tight in a way I can't shake. I'm not panicking yet, but I'm close. It's that feeling you get when you're holding something fragile and you feel it start to crack.

*Where are you?*

I've asked the question a hundred times in the last hour. But there's no her. Just silence and empty paths and the growing certainty that we fucked this up before we even had a chance to get it right.

I round the corner by the old stone benches and nearly slam into someone.

He's moving just as fast as I am. Looking around the same way—head turning, eyes scanning, body tight with the same urgency I'm carrying. He's not out for a walk. He's searching. Just like we are.

Trey.

We both pull up short. For a second we just stand there, catching our breath, sizing each other up.

We've all noticed him. Hard not to, after orientation. After the way he looked at her. None of us have said it out loud, but we're all thinking the same thing—wondering if he's part of this. Part of us. Wondering what it means if he is.

Right now, I don't care. Another set of eyes can't hurt.

I open my mouth to say something but he beats me to it.

"Have you seen her?" The question comes out rough. Desperate. Not the voice of someone who's casually concerned.

"You're—"

"Nova. Have you seen her? I need to find her."

The pieces click into place. Not just orientation. Not just proximity alerts and bureaucratic bullshit we've been ignoring. He's here. Looking for her. Covering the same ground we are.

"Fuck. So it's true."

He shakes his head, already scanning the path behind my shoulder. "I don't have time for this—"

"No. She took off this morning. We're looking too."

"Fuck." He runs a hand through his hair. The gesture is jagged, frustrated. "Silas and Harrick—"

My stomach drops.

"What did they do?"

"I don't know exactly." His voice is rough. "But whatever it was, it wasn't good. I came around the corner and she was already running. They were laughing. Harrick said something about 'she's gone, and that's all that matters.'"

I'm going to kill them.

"Come on." I turn back toward the meeting point. "This way."

He follows without arguing.

We walk fast, not quite running. I can feel him beside me—the tension radiating off him, the way he keeps scanning the paths like she might appear around any corner.

"How long have you known her?" I ask.

"I don't." He glances at me. "Not really. Just orientation. And Mark Theory—we're in the same class."

"But you're here."

"Yeah." He doesn't elaborate. Doesn't explain why he's burning bridges with his friends to chase a girl he barely knows. He doesn't have to. I can see it in the set of his jaw, the way his hands keep curling into fists.

He doesn't understand it either. But he's here anyway.

*I know the feeling.*

The others are already there when we arrive. No one's standing still—pacing, checking phones, watching the paths. The tension is visible from twenty feet away.

No Nova.

Locke sees Trey first. His whole body goes rigid. He stops pacing. His hands curl into fists at his sides.

"What the fuck is he doing here?"

Rane's head snaps up. Kyron's eyes narrow. Beckett doesn't move, but I feel his attention shift.

"Give it a rest." I step between them before anyone can move. "He's looking for Nova too."

"And we're supposed to just trust that?" Locke's voice is flat. Dangerous. He hasn't taken his eyes off Trey.

"Silas and Harrick got to her this morning," I say. "Whatever they said, it was bad enough that she ran. Trey saw the aftermath."

"Convenient." Kyron's voice is cool. "He just happened to be there."

"I told Silas to stay the fuck away from her." Trey's jaw tightens. "He told me if I walked away, I could kiss my internship goodbye. His father set the whole thing up."

"And you walked anyway," Beckett says quietly.

"I'm here, aren't I?"

Locke hasn't relaxed. "That doesn't mean we trust you."

"I'm not asking you to trust me. I'm asking you to let me help find her."

No one responds to that. Kyron shifts his weight, eyes narrowing.

"What else do you know? About Silas."

Trey exhales. "Harrick's been his usual self. But Silas... he's been different since Nova showed up."

"Different how?"

"Interested. Not in a normal way. He watches her. Asks questions about her. At first I thought it was just—" He shakes his head. "I don't know what I thought. But then I heard him on the phone."

Suddenly everyone is paying attention.

"When?" I ask.

"Three days ago. It was late. I was coming back from the training center and he was outside our building, talking to someone. I only caught pieces of it, but..." He looks at me. "He was talking about Nova. About her mark. The one she doesn't have."

"What did he say exactly?" Kyron's voice has gone sharp.

"Something about verification. About the system flagging her as an anomaly. And then he said 'father.'" Trey's jaw tightens. "That's when I knew who he was talking to."

"His father's high up in the Nightmare Order," Kyron says quietly. "Security oversight. If anyone's going to care about an unmarked anomaly, it's them." He pauses. "Which means Silas probably knows things the rest of us don't."

Trey's face shifts. "He's mentioned testing before. Some kind of program his father's involved with. I didn't think much of it at the time."

"And now?"

"Now I'm thinking about the way he looked at her."

Fuck.

I look at the others. We're all following the same thread.

Silas isn't just a bully with a grudge. He's connected to something bigger. Something that cares about Nova's missing mark enough to make phone calls about it. Something that involves testing.

"We don't have time for this," I say. "She's out there alone. Whatever Silas is doing, whoever he's talking to—none of it matters if we don't find her first."

"So where do we look?" Rane stands up. "We've already hit the main buildings."

"She's not going to show up on a fucking map," Beckett says. "She knows how to disappear."

"Then we think like her." Kyron pushes off the tree. "Where would she go if she wanted to vanish? Not hide—vanish."

"Off campus," Locke says.

"The gates are monitored."

"You think that would stop her?"

No. It wouldn't. She spent fifteen years slipping through systems designed to catch people like her. A campus gate wouldn't even slow her down.

"Twenty minutes," I say. "Go back, grab whatever you need. Who knows how long we'll be gone."

No one argues.

They scatter. Locke's already halfway across the clearing before I finish talking. Rane and Kyron head off together. Beckett pauses, looks back at me once, then goes.

Trey stands there, uncertain. Outside the formation. Not sure where he fits.

"You coming or not?"

He nods. "I know where it is. I'll meet you there."

I don't trust him. Not yet. Not fully. There's too much I don't know—about Silas, about whatever's pulling him toward Nova with the same gravity that's pulling all of us.

But she's gone. And he burned his future to come looking for her.

Right now, that makes him one of us.

# Chapter 23
## Nova

My phone's at 3%.

I've been watching it die for the last hour. Couldn't charge it even if I wanted to—no outlets in alleys, funny how that works. But I haven't been able to stop checking it either, scrolling back through messages I've read a dozen times already.

> **Locke:** Where are you?

> **Locke:** Nova.

> **Locke:** Answer your fucking phone.

> **Kyron:** We know you left. We're not angry. Just tell us you're safe.

> **Rane:** Please come back. Whatever happened, we can figure it out.

> **Beckett:** You okay?
>
> **Vaelor:** You don't have to talk. Just let us know you're alright.
>
> **Locke:** This isn't funny anymore. Where are you?
>
> **Unknown Number:** Hey. I don't know if you'll see this. I heard what happened. I'm sorry.
>
> **Unknown Number:** Oh. This is Trey by the way.

Why would he... I don't know how to add him to my phone. I should have listened better when Rane told me.

> **Rane:** I'm not mad. I promise I'm not mad. Just please answer.
>
> **Kyron:** If you need space, fine. But we need to know you're alive.
>
> **Vaelor:** We're looking for you. Not to drag you back. Just to make sure you're okay.
>
> **Locke:** If it's about... I'm sorry if I did something. If any of us did something. Just come home.
>
> **Beckett:** We miss you.
>
> **(Trey):** I told Silas to fuck off. He had no business saying anything to you. Whatever it was.

> **(Trey):** I'm with them now, Vaelor and the rest of them. Looking for you. In case that helps. Or makes it worse. I don't know.

> **Rane:** Nova please.

> **Kyron:** Wherever you are, whatever you're thinking—you're wrong. Come back.

> **Vaelor:** There's food in the fridge. Your plate. It's still there.

> **Locke:** I don't know what to do. I don't know how to fix this. Just tell me how to fix this.

> **Beckett:** Come home.

The screen flickers. 2%.

I lock the phone and press it against my chest like that'll keep it alive longer.

It won't.

The gate wasn't even hard. A gap behind the maintenance building, exactly where I would've put one if I'd designed this place. Some Academy architect clearly never slept on the streets—you learn to spot the weak points in any fence within the first six months.

That was two days ago.

I'm almost impressed with myself.

Now I'm back in the kind of places I know. Not the same streets I grew up on, but close enough. Same architecture, same instincts.

My kind of places.

The ones I don't have to read or figure out because I already understand them. Streets and people who look at me like they should—like I'm an inconvenience. Not like they did. When they looked at me like I was...

I don't know. Something.

This is where I belong.

I find a spot behind an old textile warehouse—two walls, an overhang, sightline to the street. I picked it on instinct. I've done this a thousand times. Different alleys, same geometry.

*Home sweet home.*

The thought should be funny. But it doesn't feel quite like it did before.

I settle against the wall and take inventory. No food, but I've gone longer. No jacket, which is a problem—nights are getting cold.

Phone's still at 2%.

I stop myself from reading their texts again.

I wrap my arms around myself. At least it's comfortable. The stone is cold through my pants but cold stopped being cold somewhere around year three.

This is fine. This is what I know.

So why does my chest feel like someone's sitting on it?

Day one, I tell myself it's hunger.

Day two, I know I'm lying.

The ache started small—a tightness behind my ribs that I wrote off as stress. But it's not getting better. If anything, it's getting worse. Like something's fraying inside me, thread by thread, and I can feel each one snap.

I keep moving. That's the rule. Never stay too long in one place, never get comfortable, never let anyone remember your face. I know how to do this. I've been doing this since I was eleven years old.

But my feet keep doing something wrong.

I'll pick a direction and start walking, and twenty minutes later I'll pass the same cracked sidewalk. The same graffiti tag on the corner pole. The same boarded-up shop with the faded awning.

I'm circling.

Not on purpose. But my body keeps pulling me back toward—

*Toward what?*

I know the answer. I don't want to know the answer.

I take a different route. Cut across two streets, duck through an alley I haven't used before, come out on a block I don't recognize. Good. New territory. I can work with new territory.

Fifteen minutes later, I'm back at the same fucking corner.

*What is wrong with me?*

I stop walking. Stand there in the middle of the sidewalk like an idiot, staring at the graffiti tag.

*You're losing it. You're finally, actually losing it.*

A woman pushes past me with a muttered curse. I don't move. My legs feel heavy. My chest feels heavier.

*This is withdrawal. That's all. Two weeks of regular meals and a soft bed and people who—*

*People who what?*

I close my eyes.

Locke's hands. The way they curled into fists when Harrick got too close. The way they went gentle when he touched my face.

Beckett's silence. The plate with my name on it. The way he was just *there*, every time I needed someone to be there, without making it into a thing.

Vaelor in the kitchen, adjusting my coffee. Why? I don't know. How Rane smelled when he sat too close. Kyron's eyes tracking me like he could see every thought I was trying to hide.

And—

*No.*

Trey's face. Gray eyes finding mine across a room. The brush of his arm as he passed me in Mark Theory. Too much space that felt like too much and not enough at the same time.

*He's not one of them. He's not part of this. He's—*

He's in my head anyway. Right there with the rest of them, taking up space I didn't give him permission to take.

*Fuck.*

I start walking again. Faster this time, like I can outrun it. Like distance will make the ache stop, will make the faces fade, will make my stupid body stop trying to drag me back to a place I don't belong.

*You were fine before them. You'll be fine after.*

I've been telling myself that for two days. It keeps getting less convincing.

The sun's going down by the time I admit I'm lost.

Not geographically—I know exactly where I am. Close. Too close. A few blocks from the warehouse, a couple turns from the market street. Maybe half a mile from the Academy wall.

Half a mile.

I've been walking for hours and I'm half a mile from where I started.

I stop in an alley and press my back against the wall and try to breathe. The ache in my chest has teeth now. Every inhale pulls at something raw.

*Just go back.*

The thought comes unbidden, and I shove it down so hard it should leave a bruise.

*Go back to what? To people who are probably relieved you're gone? To a room that was never really yours? To five men who were doing fine before you showed up—and probably better now that you're gone?*

*Six,* something whispers. *Six men.*

I press my palms against my eyes until I see stars.

*You don't belong there. You don't belong anywhere. That's the whole point. That's what keeps you alive.*

Fifteen years. I made it fifteen years without needing anyone.

Two weeks with them and I can't even walk in a straight line.

*Pathetic.*

I slide down the wall until I'm sitting on the cold ground, back against the stone. Same position as the warehouse. Same position as every alley, every rooftop, every forgotten corner I've called home for the last fifteen years.

The phone buzzes.

I pull it out. 1%. The screen's so dim I can barely read it.

**Beckett:** Please.

The screen goes black.

I shove the dead phone in my pocket and pull my arms tighter around myself. The cold's settling in. The light's almost gone.

I should move. Find somewhere better for the night.

I don't.

# Chapter 24
## Kyron

Walking for hours sucks, but I won't stop until I find her.

The others split off to cover more ground. I kept moving.

*If I were Nova, where would I go?*

Not the main streets. Too exposed. Not anywhere well-lit. She'd want shadows, corners, places to disappear.

I check an alley behind a row of shops. Nothing.

*Where would she feel safe?*

Stupid question. She probably doesn't feel safe anywhere. But she'd want walls at her back. A way to see who's coming before they see her.

Another alley. Empty.

*Come on, Nova. Where are you?*

I'm guessing. I know I'm guessing. I've watched her for weeks but that doesn't mean I know how she thinks, how she survives, what fifteen years on the streets actually taught her. I'm fumbling in the dark hoping I trip over something useful.

Third alley.

I almost miss her.

She's tucked against the wall, knees up, arms wrapped around herself. Small. So fucking small, folded into the shadows like she's trying to disappear.

She's not moving.

My heart stops.

I'm across the alley before I realize I'm running, on my knees beside her, hands on her face. Her skin is cold. Too cold.

"Nova."

Nothing.

"Nova, wake up."

I tap her cheek. Her head lolls.

"Come on. Look at me."

I press my fingers to her throat. Pulse. Weak, slow, but there.

She's alive.

The relief almost takes me out.

Then the anger kicks in.

"What the fuck were you thinking?"

She doesn't answer. Of course she doesn't—she's out cold. Exhaustion, exposure, probably hasn't eaten since she left. Two days out here after two weeks of actual rest. Her body forgot how to do this.

A man walks past the mouth of the alley. Looks right at us. Keeps walking.

I stare after him.

He saw her. Saw a girl on the ground in the cold and just... kept going. Like she was nothing.

Is this what it was like? For fifteen years?

A woman passes. Doesn't even glance over. A kid on a bike. Nothing. She's invisible to them.

All those years. All those nights in places like this while people walked past like she didn't exist. No wonder she doesn't know what it looks like when someone actually gives a shit.

I pull off my jacket and wrap it around her. She doesn't stir.

"I've got you," I say. Stupid, because she can't hear me. I say it anyway. "I've got you."

I get one arm under her knees, the other behind her back, and lift. She weighs nothing. That's wrong—she should weigh more, take up more space. But she's light like she's been hollowed out by years of not enough.

I start walking.

She shifts against my chest. Her head turns, pressing closer to my shoulder.

*Fuck.*

"You scared the shit out of me." My voice is rough. "Two days. Two fucking days of not knowing if you were dead in a ditch somewhere."

She doesn't answer. Her breath is shallow against my neck.

"You don't get to do that again. You hear me?"

Nothing. Just her weight in my arms and the faint warmth of her breathing.

I keep walking.

"I know you're scared. I know this is…" I shake my head. "I don't know what fifteen years of nothing looks like. I don't know how you survived it. But I know what it felt like when you walked into that house. When you looked at me."

Still nothing. But I keep talking anyway, because she can't argue back and maybe that makes me a coward but I don't care.

"You're ours, Nova. Whether you like it or not. Running doesn't change that."

A man steps out of a doorway ahead. Sees me carrying her. His lip curls—disgust, annoyance, I don't give a shit which—and he steps aside without a word.

I want to put my fist through his face.

I hold her tighter instead.

"I'm going to show you," I tell her. Quieter now. "Every day until you believe it. This is where you belong."

She shifts again. Her fingers curl into my shirt.

I stop walking.

Look down at her.

Pale. Dirty. Shadows under her eyes, lips cracked, looking like she's been through hell and back.

And she's still the most beautiful thing I've ever seen.

*There you are.*

Same thought as that first day. When she walked through the door and my whole world rearranged itself around her.

Her grip tightens on my shirt.

I start walking faster.

The house comes into view. They're all on the porch—Locke pacing, Rane gripping the railing, Vaelor standing still as stone. He sees me first. I watch his whole body lock up.

Then Locke's head snaps around.

They're running toward me before I can say anything.

"Is she—"

"Alive." My voice comes out wrecked. "Exhausted. Cold. But alive."

Locke reaches for her.

I don't let go.

"Kyron."

"I've got her."

"Let me—"

"I said I've got her."

We stare at each other. I won't fight, not with her in my arms. I get it, we both want to be the one holding her, but I'm not giving that up. Not yet.

Vaelor's hand lands on Locke's shoulder. "Let him bring her in."

Locke's jaw works. But he steps back.

I carry her up the steps, through the door, into the house. Rane's already clearing the couch, grabbing blankets. Beckett appears with water, sets it down without a word.

I don't put her down.

"Kyron." Vaelor's voice is careful. "She needs to rest."

I know. I know she does.

But her fingers are still twisted in my shirt.

"Kyron."

I lower her onto the couch. Her hand slips away and I have to stop myself from grabbing it back.

Rane tucks blankets around her. Vaelor crouches beside her, checking her pulse, murmuring something soft.

I just stand there. Watching her breathe.

Trey's in the doorway. I almost forgot about him. He looks at her, looks at me, and doesn't say anything.

He's smarter than he looks.

"She's going to be okay," Vaelor says. "Just needs rest. Food. Warmth."

"She needs to stop running," Locke says.

"She needs to know she doesn't have to," Beckett says quietly.

We all look at her. Small and pale, wrapped in blankets, finally still.

Home.

That's what she is for me. She just doesn't know it yet.

# Chapter 25
## TREY

I didn't sleep.

Not really. The chair by the window wasn't built for it—too narrow, wrong angle, it looks comfortable until you actually try to exist in it for more than ten minutes. But I stayed.

No one told me to go. That's the thing that keeps getting to me. Kyron carried her in and they all moved around her like a choreographed disaster—blankets, water, someone checking her pulse—and I just stood in the doorway like an idiot. Waiting to be asked to leave. Waiting for one of them to look at me and say *what are you still doing here?*

They didn't.

Vaelor handed me a plate around midnight. He didn't say anything. Just put food in my hands and walked away.

So I stayed. Ate food I don't remember tasting. Watched them take turns sitting with her, checking on her, doing all the things people do when someone they love is unconscious and they can't fix it.

*Love.*

I don't know if that's the right word for whatever's happening here. I don't know what the right word is. But they have it. Whatever it is. They have it and it's obvious and I'm sitting in a chair that doesn't belong to me watching something I'm not part of.

Except I couldn't leave.

Morning comes gray and slow through the window. She hasn't woken up, but something's shifted. Color in her face that wasn't there last night. The way her fingers twitched this morning when Beckett moved her blanket. She's still out, but not gone. Not like before.

Vaelor finds me in the kitchen around seven. He's making coffee, moving through the space like muscle memory, and I'm standing by the counter not sure if I should offer to help or get out of the way.

"You should eat before you go," he says without looking at me.

"I'm not hungry."

"Eat anyway."

He slides a plate across the counter. Eggs, toast, bacon. More than I deserve.

I eat because arguing seems pointless.

"She's looking better," I say. Stupid thing to say. Obvious. But I need to say something.

"She is." Vaelor pours two mugs of coffee, pushes one toward me. "Color's coming back. Pulse is stronger. She'll wake up soon."

"And then?"

He looks at me for the first time. Really looks, like he's taking my measure.

"And then we figure it out."

*We.*

He said it like I'm included. Like it's not a question.

I don't know what to do with that either.

The day drags.

I sit through three classes without hearing a word. Take notes I won't remember. Nod when people talk to me. The whole time, my head's back at the house—wondering if she's woken up, if something's changed, if I should've stayed.

By the time Mark Theory comes around, I'm wound so tight my jaw aches from clenching it.

The classroom is half-full when I get there. Same circle of chairs. Same professor arranging papers on her little table. Same everything, except—

Her seat is empty.

I knew it would be. She's unconscious on a couch across campus, surrounded by people who actually know how to take care of her. Of course she's not here.

But it still pulls at me. Like she's supposed to be there. Like some part of her still is.

I take my seat. The one across from where she usually sits. The one that lets me watch her without being obvious about it, except I'm pretty sure I've never been subtle about anything in my life.

Silas comes in two minutes before class starts.

He looks the same as always. Put together, calm, that particular brand of composure that comes from never having to doubt your place in the world. He sits down across the circle, one seat over from Nova's empty chair, and doesn't look at me.

I shouldn't say anything. I know I shouldn't. Whatever's between us now is better left alone, left to rot in silence until we can both pretend it never existed.

But her chair is empty and he's sitting there like nothing happened and I can still see Harrick's face when they laughed at her running away.

"You're lucky we found her."

The words come out before I can stop them.

Silas looks up. Slow. That flat expression I've seen a thousand times, the one that means he's calculating exactly how much you're worth to him.

"I'm sorry?"

"Nova." I keep my voice low. The professor hasn't started yet but she's watching. "You're lucky we found her when we did."

"Lucky." He tilts his head. "Why? She was back where she belongs."

My hands curl into fists on my thighs.

"She almost died."

"Did she?" He shrugs. One shoulder, casual, like we're discussing the weather. "She survived out there fifteen years. I figured she'd be fine."

He pauses and it grates at me.

"Or maybe not. Either way—" Another shrug. "She's not your problem."

I'm out of my chair before I know I'm moving.

The punch connects with his jaw. Solid, satisfying, the kind of hit that sends a message even if it costs you everything. His head snaps to the side and for one perfect second he looks surprised.

Then the professor is shouting and someone's grabbing my arm and Silas is just sitting there, hand on his jaw, watching me with something that looks almost like amusement.

He doesn't swing back. Doesn't even stand up.

That's worse somehow.

"Both of you. Out. Now."

The professor's voice cuts through the chaos. I'm breathing hard, knuckles throbbing, and Silas is already rising from his chair like this is all mildly inconvenient.

We end up in the hallway. The door shuts behind us and it's just the two of us now, no witnesses, no buffer.

Silas brushes off his shirt. Straightens his collar. Doesn't touch his jaw even though I know it's going to bruise.

"That's it, Trey. We're done."

"We were done the second you made her cry."

"No. We were done the second you decided she mattered more than your future." He straightens his collar. "My father was disappointed, by the way. When I told him you weren't interested anymore. He had such high hopes for you."

I don't say anything. I made my choice three days ago.

"And when he comes for her," Silas says, softer now, almost gentle, "I'll be the one helping him."

The world narrows.

"When he *what*?"

"You didn't think this was just about you, did you?" He takes a step back. Smiling now. "She's an anomaly, Trey. An unmarked adult who slipped through the system for fifteen years. My father's very interested in understanding how that happened."

"You stay the fuck away from her."

"Or what? You'll hit me again?" He laughs. Short, sharp. "Pathetic."

I lunge.

And then there are hands on me—two sets, grabbing my arms, hauling me back. I'm fighting them without thinking, still trying to reach Silas, still trying to—

"Trey. *Trey*. Stop."

Locke's voice. Low and hard in my ear. His grip is iron on my arm.

Rane's got my other side, pushing himself between me and Silas. "Walk away," he says to Silas. "Now."

Silas doesn't move. He's looking at all three of us with an expression I can't read.

"You're the ones running out of time," he says. "Remember that."

Then he turns and walks away. Unhurried. Like he didn't just say he was going to help his father.

Locke doesn't let go until Silas rounds the corner.

"What the fuck was that?" Rane's voice is tight. "What did he mean, *when he comes for her?*"

I'm still shaking. Still trying to breathe through the rage that's sitting in my chest like its trying to claw its way out.

"He wasn't talking," I manage. "That was a promise."

Rane's face goes pale. "We knew his father was watching. Gathering information. But this—"

"This is different." Locke's jaw is tight.

We stand there for a second, the three of us, the hallway empty and too quiet.

"Can we leave?" The question comes out before I think it through. "If the system's actually coming for her—can we just go?"

"Go where?" Rane shakes his head. "The Houses control everything. Every territory, every border. You can't just disappear."

"She did. For fifteen years."

"And look what it cost her."

Silence.

"What does 'coming for her' even mean?" I ask. "Containment? Testing? What are we actually dealing with?"

"We don't know." Locke starts walking. We follow. "That's the problem. We don't know what his father wants, what the Nightmare Order's interest is, or how much time we have."

"So we figure it out," Rane says. "We keep her close. We don't let her out of our sight."

"And if we can't figure it out in time?" I ask.

Neither of them answers.

The house comes into view. From the outside, everything looks peaceful. But I know better.

"We don't let her out of our sight," I say again. Quieter now. "Not again."

Locke glances at me. Something shifts in his expression—not quite acceptance, but close.

"Agreed."

As we walk inside, Vaelor's coming down the stairs. He stops when he sees us. Kyron's leaning against the kitchen doorway with a mug, and Beckett's on the couch next to—

She's sitting up.

Blanket pooled around her waist, pale hair tangled, shadows still under her eyes. Beckett's saying something to her, low enough that I can't hear it. She's nodding along, but then the door closes behind us and her head turns.

She sees me.

Those pale blue eyes lock onto mine and don't let go.

And then she smiles—small, almost nothing—and looks away like she didn't mean to do it.

I grip the doorframe without meaning to. Just to keep from falling forward. Or maybe just to keep my shit together.

Everything I've been carrying for three days—the guilt, the anger, the pull I couldn't explain—it all goes quiet. Just for a second. Just long enough for me to understand what I've been trying not to know.

I'm not fighting this anymore.

I don't know what I am to her. I don't know what I am to any of them. But I know I'm not leaving.

Not now. Not ever.

She's awake. She's looking at me.

And I can't pretend I don't feel it anymore.

# Chapter 26
## Nova

I don't know where I am at first.

Warm. That's the only thing that registers. Warm and soft and something smells like coffee and I'm not cold, I'm not on concrete, I'm not—

The ceiling comes into focus. White. Clean.

The house.

I turn my head and my neck aches, my whole body aches, but in a distant way. Like the pain belongs to someone else and I'm just borrowing it.

Beckett's sitting on the floor near the window, back against the wall, scrolling through his phone. He looks up when I move. Doesn't say anything. Holds my gaze for a second, then nods.

*You're okay. You're here.*

That's it.

I try to sit up and my arms shake. I make it halfway before I have to stop, breathing hard, which is embarrassing. I used to walk ten miles on an empty stomach. Now I can't even sit up without my body staging a protest.

Beckett sets his phone down. "Take your time."

"I'm fine."

"You're not." There's no judgment in it. "But you will be."

I manage to get upright. The blanket pools around my waist and I realize I'm still in the same clothes I was wearing when I—

When I what?

The alley. The cold. My phone dying. And then... nothing. Flashes. Warmth. Being carried. A voice in my ear I couldn't quite hold onto.

"How long was I out?"

"Since last night. It's almost five now."

Almost a full day. I've lost a full day.

"Where is everyone?"

"Kyron's in the kitchen." I glance over—he's leaning against the doorway with a mug, watching me with those sharp blue eyes. He lifts the mug slightly in greeting. "Vaelor's upstairs charging your phone. Locke and Rane had class." Beckett pauses. "Trey's been with them. They should be back soon."

Footsteps on the stairs. Beckett stops talking.

Vaelor appears with a sleeve of crackers in one hand and a glass of water in the other. My phone is tucked in his pocket, charging cable trailing.

"Finally got enough juice to turn on," he says, setting them on the coffee table. Then he looks at me—really looks—and something shifts in his face. Relief, or something close to it.

"You're awake."

"Apparently."

He pulls the phone from his pocket and sets it beside the crackers. "Figured you'd want it back."

"Eat," he says. "Slow. See if you can keep it down."

"I'm not—"

My stomach growls. Loud enough that all four of us hear it.

Vaelor's mouth twitches. "You were saying?"

I stick my tongue out at him. Pick up a cracker anyway.

I make myself go slow even though my body wants to inhale everything in sight. One cracker. Sip of water. Another cracker. Vaelor watches without commenting, and I'm halfway through the sleeve when I feel it. That prickle at the back of my neck.

I look up.

Vaelor's watching me. Not the food. Me.

I take another bite. His eyes follow the movement.

"What?"

"Nothing." But his voice is lower than it was a second ago. "Glad you're eating."

I take another bite and his gaze tracks to my mouth and—oh.

*Oh.*

I shove another cracker in because it's easier than figuring out what my face is doing.

I finish what I can. Set the rest down. My stomach feels strange—not full, but not empty. Something in between.

Beckett moves from his spot by the window. Takes the glass from me, sets it on the coffee table, then settles on the floor near the couch.

"How you feeling?"

"Fine."

He gives me a look. The kind that says he's not buying it.

"Nova. You don't have to be brave with us. You can tell us what's going on."

I take a breath. Something in my chest loosens, just a little. "I'm just—"

The door opens.

"She's up," Beckett says without turning around.

Voices in the hallway, the thud of bags being dropped, footsteps. And then they're coming through together. Rane first, moving fast, pulling up short at the edge of the couch. My skin remembers his chest against my shoulder. The way I leaned into him without meaning to.

Locke behind him, stopping in the doorway. Arms crossed. Jaw tight.

And suddenly I'm back on those steps. His hand on my face. His mouth on mine. The sound he made against my lips—

My whole body flushes hot.

I look away so fast I almost give myself whiplash. Stare at my hands like they're the most interesting things I've ever seen. My heart is pounding and I don't know if it's from the memory or from him being *right there* and we haven't talked about it and everyone probably knows and—

There's movement behind Locke, and I lift my head to look again.

Trey.

He edges past Locke into the room, and his eyes find mine.

I think I stop breathing.

I smile before I can stop myself. And then I look away because I didn't mean to do that. My face is warm again.

*Why does my face keep doing that?*

I catch Rane and Kyron exchanging a look I can't read.

"How are you feeling?" Rane's voice. I grab onto it like a lifeline.

"Better." I risk a glance up. Not at Locke. At Rane. "Thanks."

"You scared the shit out of us." He says it lightly, but something underneath isn't light at all.

"I know. I'm—"

"Don't apologize." Kyron pushes off from the doorway, moving into the room. "Just don't do it again."

I nod trying not to think about what that means.

"So," Rane says into the silence. "We should probably talk about—"

"Not tonight." Beckett's voice is quiet but firm.

Rane opens his mouth. Closes it.

"He's right," Kyron says. "It can wait."

"We'll still be here tomorrow," Vaelor adds. "All of it will still be here tomorrow."

I watch Locke's jaw work. He wants to push. I can see it in every line of his body. But he doesn't.

"Fine," he says. "Tomorrow."

Rane rocks back on his heels, shoves his hands in his pockets.

"So... dinner?"

And suddenly they're moving.

Rane disappears into the kitchen and comes back with plates. Vaelor follows him and returns with more food—enough for everyone, like he'd been planning for this. Kyron grabs silverware. Locke moves one of the chairs closer without being asked.

And Trey—

Trey settles onto the floor with his back against the couch.

Right next to my legs.

Close enough that if I shifted my knee, I'd touch his shoulder. Close enough that I can feel the warmth of him through the blanket. He doesn't look at me when he does it. Just drops down like that's where he belongs and starts eating.

My skin is humming.

I stay on the couch, legs tucked under me, plate balanced on my knees. I'm hyperaware of every inch of space between my leg and his shoulder. The urge to move closer wars with the urge to climb over the back of the couch and flee.

I do neither. I sit there, trying to remember how to eat.

"Our girl's finally got some color back," Rane says, and something in my chest stutters.

*Our girl.*

The words hang in the room. No one corrects him.

I shove a forkful of food into my mouth so I don't have to respond.

"You should've seen Rane while we were looking for you," Kyron says. He's on the floor by the window now, plate balanced on one knee. "Insufferable."

"Like you were any better," Rane fires back. "Mr. 'Let's check that alley again for the fourth time.'"

"We all wanted to check it again," Vaelor says quietly.

I keep my eyes on my plate. My face feels like it's on fire.

"Okay," Rane says, too loud, clearly trying to reset. "Someone tell me something that isn't about the last three days. I'm begging."

"You could try not talking with your mouth open," Kyron says.

"I could. I won't, but I could."

"Disgusting."

"Thank you, I try."

Vaelor shakes his head, but he's smiling. "Remember when Rane tried to cook for the first time?"

"We don't talk about that," Rane says immediately.

"We absolutely talk about that." Kyron's mouth curves. "The fire department talked about it."

"There was no fire department."

"There was *almost* a fire department."

"Almost doesn't count."

I take a bite of food so I don't have to figure out what to say. They're bickering like brothers, and I don't know how to join in. But I don't feel like I have to, either.

Trey shifts against the couch. I feel the movement more than see it—the brush of his shoulder against the cushion near my knee. My breath catches.

He heard it. I know he heard it because he goes still.

Neither of us moves.

"I used to go to this place," Trey says.

The conversation stutters. Everyone looks at him.

He's staring at his plate, turning his fork over in his fingers.

"Near the border of Reverie and Dreams. There's this—I don't know how to describe it. A courtyard, kind of. Old buildings around it. Felt like no one had used it in years." He shrugs, still not looking up. "I kept ending up there. I don't know why. I'd tell myself I was going somewhere else and then I'd just... be there."

Silence.

Kyron sets his plate down slowly. "Where exactly?"

"South side of the neutral zone. There's a fountain that doesn't work anymore. Stone benches."

"Holy shit." Rane's voice has gone strange. "That's—"

"That's where we met," Locke finishes. His voice is flat, but something underneath it isn't flat at all. "All of us. That's the spot."

Trey's head comes up. "What?"

"Four years ago. That's where we kept running into each other." Kyron's blue eyes are sharp, calculating. "Before the system flagged us. Before any of this. That courtyard."

"I was there," Trey says slowly. "Four years ago. I was there all the time."

"We never saw you."

"I never saw you either."

My fork is halfway to my mouth. I set it down.

The courtyard. The neutral zone between Reverie and Dreams. Old buildings. A broken fountain.

I know that place.

I know that place because I spent three weeks sleeping behind one of those old buildings. Because the fountain had a ledge that blocked the wind. Because I used to sit on those stone benches in the early morning before anyone else was awake and watch the sky turn gray.

Four years ago.

"Nova?"

Someone's saying my name. I don't know who. I'm too busy trying to breathe around the thing that's lodged itself in my chest.

"Nova, you okay?"

I look up. They're all watching me now. Six faces, six different expressions of concern.

"That was a really dark time for me," I hear myself say.

My voice doesn't sound like mine. Too quiet. Too far away.

"What do you mean?" Rane asks.

I swallow. My throat is tight.

"I think I was there too."

Heavier silence now.

"Four years ago?" Kyron's voice is careful.

I nod. "I stayed there for a few weeks. Behind one of the buildings. There was this ledge by the fountain that blocked the wind." I'm looking at my hands, at the plate I'm no longer holding because at some point I set it down. "I remember the benches. I used to sit there before dawn."

"I didn't see any of you," I say. "I would have remembered."

"We were usually there in the evenings," Vaelor says slowly. "After training hours."

"I was always gone by then. It wasn't safe to stay in one place during the day."

The math is happening in all of their heads. I can see it. Four years ago, they were being pulled to the same spot. Finding each other. Starting something none of them understood.

And I was there too. Sleeping in the margins. Surviving. Never knowing that the people I was apparently supposed to belong to were twenty feet away.

"Fuck," Rane breathes.

"Yeah," I say. "Pretty much."

Trey shifts against the couch, his whole body has gone tense.

"We were all there," he says. "All seven of us. Four years before any of this."

"The system didn't catch it," Kyron says. "They flagged five of us, but they missed you." He's looking at Trey. "And they definitely missed her."

"She wasn't in the system," Locke says. "She couldn't be flagged."

"Neither could I. Not for that." Trey's voice is rough. "My mark was already messed up. They weren't looking at me the same way they were looking at you."

I don't say anything. I'm still trying to wrap my head around it—all of us, in the same place, at the same time.

We never even knew.

"This is fucked up," Rane says, but there's no heat in it. Just exhaustion. "This is really, really fucked up."

"It's something," Vaelor agrees quietly.

The conversation doesn't pick back up after that. Not really. Rane clears the plates. He goes to the kitchen and comes back without them. Kyron asks if anyone wants anything. Normal things. Quiet things.

But no one leaves.

Rane puts music on—something low and soft, barely there. Vaelor dims the lights. Kyron stretches out on the floor with his arm behind his head, staring at the ceiling.

Trey stays where he is. Back against the couch. Close enough that I can feel the warmth of him through the blanket.

I curl deeper into the cushions and watch them settle in around me.

Locke's still in the chair, but his posture has softened. His eyes are closed, though I don't think he's sleeping. Beckett's head is tipped back against the wall.

I keep waiting for someone to get up. To say goodnight. To go to their room.

No one does.

Rane stretches out on the floor near Kyron. Vaelor shifts in the armchair, getting comfortable. Trey's breathing has gone slow and even against the couch.

They're staying.

All of them. Here. With me.

"Same time tomorrow?" Rane murmurs from somewhere to my left.

A few murmurs of agreement. Someone might have said *yeah*. Someone else might have grunted.

I don't know if they're talking to me.

But I hope they are.

My eyes are getting heavy. The warmth is soaking into my bones—not just from the blanket, but from them. From being surrounded. From knowing that if I close my eyes, they'll still be here when I open them.

For the first time in fifteen years, I don't feel like I need to watch the door.

I close my eyes.

The door's right there. I don't look at it once.

# Chapter 27
## NOVA

I wake up slowly.

I lay there with my eyes closed. My body feels better than it did yesterday, less ache and more... warmth. Solid warmth everywhere.

My hand.

Someone is holding it. Fingers laced through mine, palm pressed against palm, and I don't remember reaching for anyone but here we are.

I open my eyes.

Trey.

He's turned toward the couch sometime in the night, hip pressed against it, arm across the cushion with his fingers wrapped around mine. His cheek rests on his forearm, face inches from where my hand lies.

I should pull away. I should—

But his skin is warm and his grip is loose and something about it feels *right* in a way that settles into my chest instead of making me panic.

I look at his face.

He's already watching me. Gray eyes half-lidded, mouth curved up at one corner like he's been waiting for me to notice.

"Hey," he says. Barely a whisper.

"Hey."

He pushes up on his free arm, leans in. Stops. Like he's checking to see if I'll run.

I don't.

His nose bumps mine and I smile before I can stop it. And then his mouth finds mine and it's softer than I expected. Tentative. I let myself sink into it.

He makes a small sound against my lips, surprised, and I feel him smile into the kiss—

Someone shifts.

I pull back. Turn.

They're all awake. Every single one of them. Watching.

*Oh god.*

My face floods with heat. I'm already pulling my hand free, already trying to figure out how to explain, how to apologize, how to—

"Nova."

Locke's voice. Low. Steady.

I make myself look at him. He's still in the chair, eyes half-lidded, expression unreadable.

"You don't need permission to act on what you feel. Not with us."

I stare at him.

"What?" My voice comes out wrong. Too high. "You can't be serious. I mean you guys can't all—"

I look around the room. They're all watching me. Something in their eyes I don't understand. Something that looks like—

I'm on my feet before I decide to stand. My legs are shaky but they hold.

"Shoes. Where are my shoes?"

"Nova—"

"Where are—"

Rane sets them down by my feet. Doesn't say anything.

"Thanks."

I shove them on, fingers clumsy.

"Nova, you can't leave." Vaelor's voice. Careful. "Not again."

"I'm not."

"Nova—"

"I'm *not*. I'm going for a walk. I just—I can't—I don't know what—" I make a sound that's not quite a word. "I need air."

I'm out the door before anyone can stop me.

The morning is cold and gray and I don't care. I just need to move, need to think, need to figure out what the fuck is happening and why they're all looking at me like—

"Stop."

Kyron's voice. Twenty feet behind me.

I don't stop.

"Nova."

"I can't."

"You can turn around."

"I can't do that either."

"Why?"

I keep walking. He keeps following. I can hear his footsteps, steady, unhurried. Like he's got all the time in the world.

"Because I can't let you go." His voice is closer now. "Not anymore."

I stop.

I don't want to. My legs just stop moving.

I turn around.

He's standing there, dark hair messy from sleep, those blue eyes fixed on me like I'm the only thing that exists.

"What do you want?" The words come out sharper than I mean them to.

He blinks. "What?"

"What do you *want* from me?" I'm getting louder and I can't stop it. "People don't do this. People don't just give you food and kindness for no reason. And if you think I'm going to—that I'll just—"

"No." He cuts me off. "Not like that, Nova."

"Then what's it like?"

He runs his hands through his hair. For a second he looks almost lost, and that's wrong—Kyron's never lost, Kyron always knows exactly what's happening—

"You're ours, Nova." He says it simply. Like it's obvious. "Rane said it last night. No one corrected him because it's true."

I open my mouth. Nothing comes out.

"It's not just the system. Not just a cluster label." He takes a step closer. "We knew. All of us. The moment we saw you."

"But what does that even mean, Kyron?"

He doesn't answer. Just watches me with those impossible blue eyes.

"I had never even heard of a cluster until a few weeks ago. I don't understand why the woman who did my makeup when Zoe and I were shopping kept talking about it like it was something every woman wanted. Why she was so happy about her own and kept telling me how lucky I was."

I take a breath because I have to get this out.

"And you guys are just *there*. Walking me to class. Making sure I have things. Fuck, you paid—" My voice cracks. "You paid for me to go shopping. And I got the softest sweater and creams that Zoe said I needed and I don't even know *why* and... and..."

I finally stop talking and look at him.

He's beaming. Not a smirk, not that knowing look he usually wears. A real smile, huge, reaching his eyes.

"You're perfect," he breathes, and steps closer.

I don't step back. I roll my eyes without meaning to.

"Nova." He steps forward again, his hand coming up, thumb brushing my cheek. "We want to do those things for you. It's not fake. It's not a burden."

His palm settles against my jaw, tilting my face up toward his.

"We want to see you happy and fed and safe. And we want to be here while you figure out who you are and who you could be."

And then he kisses me.

Not like Trey—soft and tentative and asking. Not like Locke—overwhelming, barely restrained, a claiming.

Kyron kisses me like he's been thinking about it for weeks. Like he's had a plan and he's finally executing it. Precise and deliberate and *thorough*.

My hands find his shirt without permission. Fist in the fabric. Pull him closer.

My breath catches, and then his other hand is in my hair and he's tilting my head back and there's nothing else. Just the slide of his mouth against mine, the way he tastes, the sound of my own heartbeat drowning out everything.

I'm just *here*. In this. Wanting this.

*Wanting him.*

The realization doesn't scare me like it probably should. It settles and stays there, warm and terrifying and undeniable.

I want this. I want *them*.

When we finally break apart, we're both breathing hard. His forehead drops against mine, his hand still cradling my jaw, his thumb tracing my cheekbone.

"Oh," I say. Stupid. The only word I can find.

He laughs. Low and warm, breath fanning across my lips.

"Yeah," he says. "Oh."

# Chapter 28
## LOCKE

I'm on the porch when I see them.

Kyron's walking back toward the house. Slow. Unsteady. And it takes me a second to figure out why—

Nova.

Her legs are wrapped around his waist. Her arms around his neck. And they're kissing. Not coming up for air, not looking where they're going, just *kissing* while he stumbles toward the steps like a drunk man trying to find his front door.

I thought this would bother me.

I kissed her first. I've been replaying it in my head for days—her lips, the sound she made, the way she ran. I thought seeing her with one of the others would twist something in my chest. Jealousy or possessiveness. Something ugly I'd have to swallow down.

But watching Kyron carry her across the yard, watching her hands fist in his hair, watching her *choose* this—

I don't feel jealous.

Not really.

I just want it to be me.

*Huh.*

And then the other feeling hits. Deeper. Darker.

*Mine. Ours. Finally.*

"Guys."

I don't turn around. Don't need to. I hear them moving behind me, filtering out onto the porch.

"Well, son of a bitch." Rane's voice.

"Right?"

"That can't be Nova." Trey, sounding dazed.

"But it is."

Silence. We all watch them get closer. Kyron nearly trips on a root. Nova doesn't even flinch—just keeps kissing him like she doesn't care if he falls.

"Guys." Vaelor's voice is careful. "Did we—is this really the start of—"

"Yeah." I nod slowly. "Yeah, it is."

More silence. The good kind. Because we're all standing here watching them like we did that first day she showed up.

Like idiots.

"Hey." Beckett's voice cuts through, quiet but firm. "This doesn't change anything. Not really."

I glance at him.

"She's still terrified," he says. "Still adjusting. We still have to take it slow."

He's right. I know he's right. One kiss—three kisses—doesn't undo fifteen years of survival mode. Doesn't mean she trusts us. Doesn't mean she won't bolt again the next time something scares her.

I nod. "Agreed."

They're almost to the steps now. Kyron's grinning against her mouth, barely watching where he's going. Nova still hasn't looked up.

Rane starts clapping.

Then Trey. Then Vaelor. Beckett whistles, sharp and loud.

Nova freezes.

Her head whips around and she sees us—all of us, lined up on the porch, applauding like she just won something—and her face goes so red I can see it from here.

She buries her face in Kyron's neck.

He's laughing, one hand coming up to cradle the back of her head, still holding her up with the other arm. "It's okay," I hear him say. "You're okay."

She mumbles something into his shoulder. He laughs harder.

"What'd she say?" Rane calls out.

"She said she hates all of you."

"Fair enough."

Kyron carries her up the steps. She still won't look at us, face hidden, ears bright red. He's stroking her hair, murmuring something I can't hear, and the way she melts into him—

*Mine. Ours. Hers.*

"Nova."

She tenses at my voice. Lifts her head just enough to peek at me with one eye.

"Welcome back," I say.

She groans and buries her face again.

# Chapter 29
## Nova

Two weeks.

Two weeks of waking up in a house that's starting to feel like mine. Two weeks of meals I don't have to hide to eat. Two weeks of walking to class with people on all sides of me—not boxing me in, just… there.

I'm wearing the green sweater. The soft one Zoe made me buy. It still feels strange, owning something this nice. But every time I put it on, I feel more comfortable in my own skin than I ever have.

"That color looks good on you."

Kyron falls into step beside me. His eyes drag down to the sweater, then back up to my face. Slow and deliberate.

My face goes warm. Too warm. I blame the morning air. I blame him.

"Thanks," I manage.

His mouth curves. He knows exactly what he's doing.

Trey's waiting at the end of the path like he has been every morning for the past two weeks. He should just have a room at this point. I don't say it, but I think it every time I see him standing there, hands in his pockets, scanning the path until he spots us.

Spots me.

His shoulders drop when our eyes meet. Like he was holding his breath until he knew I was there.

I don't know what to do with that. So I don't do anything. Just let Rane bump my shoulder as we reach Trey, let Vaelor's hand brush my back as the group shifts to absorb him.

Always in the middle. I've stopped fighting it.

"You okay?" I ask Trey. He looks distracted. More than usual.

"Yeah. Just—" He shakes his head. "Silas has been weird lately."

"Weird how?"

"Haven't seen him much. And when I do, he's..." He trails off, searching for the word. "Quiet. Watching. More than usual."

"That's not ominous at all," Rane mutters.

"He's always watching," Locke says. Flat. "That's not new."

"This feels different."

No one argues with that.

We keep walking. The morning air is crisp, the kind of cold that wakes you up without biting. Students drift past alone and in groups, everyone heading the same direction. It's nice, how normal it is.

"Nova!"

I turn. Zoe's crossing the quad toward us, two of her guys trailing behind. Eli, and one I don't recognize—tall, dark hair, moving like he's aware of every angle around him.

"Hey." She falls into step beside me, her guys peeling off to join mine. I glance back and they're already talking—low voices, easy postures, like they've known each other for years.

Maybe they have. I'm still learning how all of this works.

"How are you doing?" Zoe asks.

If there's one thing I've learned about Zoe, she means it.

"Good. Better." I hesitate. "It's getting easier."

She smiles. "Told you."

We walk in comfortable silence for a minute. The guys are a loose orbit around us—not hovering, thank goodness. I've stopped noticing how they rotate, how there's always someone at my shoulder, my back, my blind spots. It used to make me twitchy. Now it just feels like... how things are.

The sound comes first.

Engines. Low, rumbling, wrong.

I stop walking. So does everyone else.

Three black vehicles are pulling through the main gate. Not cars—bigger, armored, with tinted windows that catch the light like oil. They move slowly, deliberately, like they have every right to be here.

"What the hell?" Rane's voice is tight.

"That's... strange, right?" I look at Kyron. "Tell me that's strange."

"It's strange." His eyes haven't left the vehicles. "No one has vehicles except Nightmare Order. It's one of the ways they control movement between territories."

"And they don't come here," Beckett adds. "Academy's supposed to be neutral ground. High-level oversight only."

The vehicles roll past us, heading toward the administrative building. Students stop and stare. Conversations die mid-sentence.

"If they're on campus," Zoe murmurs, "something's already broken."

No one argues.

"Trey." Locke's voice is low. "You think this has anything to do with Silas?"

Trey's jaw tightens. "I don't know. Maybe."

"Wait—Silas?" Zoe glances between us. "What's going on with Silas?"

"He's had his eye on Nova," Locke says.

"Shit." Zoe's expression darkens. "Since when?"

"Since she got here," Rane says. "It's been... a thing."

"We're handling it," Vaelor adds quietly.

Zoe's expression hardens. "That guy's an asshole. Doesn't help that he hides behind his daddy for everything. It's like he's untouchable."

Murmurs of agreement from the guys. All of them—mine and hers.

"Well." Eli crosses his arms, watching the vehicles disappear around a corner. "Better be on our best behavior."

"Right," Rane says. "Because that's our specialty."

A few laughs. Tight, and a little nervous.

The tension doesn't break, but it eases. Enough to keep moving.

"Come on," Kyron says. "We'll be late."

We head to class.

But I look back once. The vehicles are parked now. Figures in dark uniforms climbing out, moving toward the building with purpose.

Something cold settles in my stomach.

It's starting.

I don't know what *it* is yet. But I can feel it.

# Chapter 30
## NOVA

The man in black is sitting in the back of the classroom.

I notice him the second we walk in. Vaelor does too—I feel his hand press briefly against my lower back, guiding me toward the front.

We don't sit in the back today.

As we pass, the man's eyes find mine. Lock on. Don't let go.

Something crosses his face. Disgust. Like I'm something he scraped off his shoe.

I look away first. I hate that I do.

We take seats near the front. I'm still shivering when I sit down.

"Hey." Vaelor leans over, voice low. "You alright?"

"Yeah. That guy, he's…"

"Yeah. I know." His jaw is tight. "I saw it."

"What do you think—"

"I don't know. But we'll figure it out." He holds my gaze. Steady. Sure. "Don't worry."

I nod. Try to believe him.

First vehicles show up a few days ago, now this?

*What the hell is going on?*

Class starts and I don't hear a word of it.

The professor is talking about resonance theory—something about frequency alignment and proximity effects—but the words slide right past me. All I can feel is the weight of eyes on the back of my neck.

Vaelor shifts beside me. His shoulder presses against mine and stays there.

He doesn't look at me. Doesn't say anything. Just... leans in. Solid and warm and *there*.

Some of the tension bleeds out of me and I lean into it.

I keep waiting for something to happen. For the man in the back to stand up, to say something, to point at me and announce whatever crime I've committed by existing.

He doesn't. He just sits there. Watching.

Halfway through class, the weight disappears.

I don't turn around to check. But I know. The air feels different. Lighter.

When class ends, I glance back.

The seat is empty. He's gone.

The relief lasts about three seconds before the unease settles back in. He left. But he saw what he came to see.

"Come on." Vaelor's hand finds my back again. "Let's get lunch. I'll meet you at the table—need to drop something off first."

I nod.

The dining hall is loud and bright and full of food.

I'm still not used to it. Two weeks of meals here and my brain still short-circuits every time I see the spread—stations for everything, trays piled high, people just... taking what they want. Like it's nothing.

I grab a plate. Move through the line slowly, trying to actually think about what I want instead of what will keep me alive the longest.

There's bread at the end of the station. Fresh, warm, the kind I used to grab first because it was filling and kept well and didn't matter if it got stale.

I pass it.

I grab fruit instead. Some kind of pasta. A piece of chicken that looks actually seasoned for once.

It feels like a small victory. Choosing what I want instead of what I need.

I turn toward our usual table and spot them immediately. All of them except Vaelor—Locke at the end, Trey across from him, Rane and Kyron in the middle, Beckett with his back to the wall.

Locke's eyes find mine across the room. Something in his expression softens.

I start walking toward them.

And then Silas steps into my path.

He's just *there*, like he materialized out of the crowd. That same smile. That same look in his eyes that makes my skin crawl.

"So it's true," he says. "You're back."

I don't respond. I shift my plate to one hand and try to step around him.

He moves with me. Blocking my path.

I go the other way. He mirrors it, smooth and unhurried, like we're dancing and he's leading.

My grip tightens on the plate. "Excuse me."

"In a hurry?" He doesn't move. "That's a shame. We haven't caught up in so long."

"We've never caught up. We've never had a conversation." I step left. He steps left. My jaw clenches. "Move."

His smile widens. Like my anger is exactly what he wanted.

"There she is." He tilts his head, studying me. "I was starting to think they'd housebroken you."

I hold back a scoff.

"You can't stop and talk to an old friend?" His smirk widens. "That's rude."

"We're not friends."

"No?" He tilts his head. "That's too bad."

He pauses. Looks down at me. Something shifts in his expression—darker, sharper.

Then he leans in.

His breath is warm against my ear. His voice is barely a whisper.

"They're coming for you."

I freeze.

"Say anything, and they'll stop pretending your men are innocent."

He pulls back. Smiling again. Like he didn't just—

"What are you talking about?"

He smiles like it's a secret he's looking forward to watching me learn.

"You'll see."

"Is there a problem here?"

Trey's voice. I turn and he's right there, Locke and Rane flanking him. All three of them looking at Silas like they're deciding how many pieces to leave behind.

"No." Silas's smile doesn't waver. "No problem at all. Right, Nova?"

My throat is tight. I shake my head. "No. No problem."

"Good."

They lead me to the table and I let them. My legs feel like they're made of something that isn't quite solid.

I can feel Silas watching. I don't look back, but I know. That sneer. Those eyes.

Then he's gone.

My skin is too hot. My chest too tight. I blame the adrenaline. I tell myself it's fear.

The burn doesn't fade.

"What the fuck was that about?" Rane asks as I sit down.

I stare at my plate. "I ran into him again. Literally. I wasn't paying attention."

It's the truth. Just not the whole one.

Locke's watching me. That flat, assessing look that sees too much.

"Nova."

"It's fine."

"It didn't look fine."

"He's just—" I push a piece of pasta around my plate. "He's Silas. He's always like that."

"Like what?" Trey's voice is tight. "Because from where I was standing, it looked like he was threatening you."

I open my mouth.

*Say anything, and they'll stop pretending your men are innocent.*

I close it.

Beckett's watching me. I catch his eye and see it there—the disappointment. Like he knows I'm holding something back and he's waiting for me to trust them enough to let it out.

I look away.

"It's fine, guys." I put my fork down. "Really."

No one says anything for a long moment.

Then Vaelor slides into the seat beside me. He takes one look at my face, at the tension around the table, and his jaw tightens.

"What happened?"

"Silas," Locke says.

"Again?"

"Yeah."

Vaelor's hand finds my knee under the table. Squeezes once.

"Speaking of unwelcome attention," he says slowly, "there was a man in our class today. Back of the room. Nightmare Order, from the look of him. He spent the whole time he was there staring at Nova."

The table goes quiet.

"Same here." Kyron's voice is flat. "Different class. Same setup. Guy in black, back corner, watching."

"Us too," Rane says. He glances at Beckett, who nods.

"They were in all of our classes?" I ask.

"Looks like it."

I push my plate away. My appetite is gone.

"So they're watching all of us now."

"They're watching *you*." Locke's voice is hard. "We're just in the way."

*Say anything, and they'll stop pretending your men are innocent.*

The burn in my chest spreads.

I don't say anything.

And I pretend I don't notice the way they all watch me like they're waiting for something to break.

# Chapter 31
## NOVA

Saturday afternoon is quiet.

I'm on the floor, stomach down, textbook open in front of me. Something about territorial boundary laws and cross-House jurisdiction. The words keep blurring together.

Locke checks the clock on the wall. Third time in ten minutes.

Kyron drops down beside me. Too close. His shoulder brushes mine as he leans over to look at what I'm working on.

"You're overthinking it," he says. "The answer's in the third paragraph."

"I read the third paragraph."

"Read it again."

I huff but look down. He shifts closer, pointing at a line halfway down the page. His arm presses against mine.

Heat hits low and sharp but I'm not embarrassed. This feels like something else entirely.

My pen slips. I pretend it's nothing.

"See it now?" His voice is low. Close to my ear.

"Yep. Got it. Thanks."

He doesn't move away.

Beckett's pacing between the kitchen and the living room like he can't decide where to land. Trey adjusts his shirt. Again.

The clock on the wall ticks past five.

I don't notice at first—I'm still trying to focus on the words in front of me—but the energy changes. Restless, almost expectant as something shifts in the room.

"Maybe we should call it on homework, huh?" Vaelor's voice from somewhere behind me.

"Nah, I wanna finish this." I flip a page. "Just get it over with so I can relax, you know?"

"It'll be there tomorrow, Nova."

"I know, but I just wanna get it done."

I hear footsteps on the stairs. Don't look up.

"Nova?"

"Hmm?" Still reading. Or trying to.

Someone clears their throat. "Nova."

Something in the tone makes me finally lift my head.

Rane is standing at the bottom of the stairs.

He's... dressed up. Button-down shirt, sleeves rolled to his elbows. Hair actually styled instead of its usual mess. He looks good. Really good.

I sit up slowly. "What's going on? Why do you look like that?"

His face goes red. Behind me, someone snorts. Someone else mutters something I don't catch.

"Oh, well, I—" He clears his throat again. Shoves his hands in his pockets, pulls them out, doesn't seem to know what to do with them. "I was hoping... maybe..."

He takes a breath.

"Nova... would you do me the honor of letting me take you to dinner?"

Someone groans from the couch. "Jesus, Rane, did you black out and wake up in a regency novel?"

"Shut up," Rane mutters, ears going pink.

I blink at him.

"Don't we usually eat here?"

A noise from behind me—Kyron choking on something, Locke's low laugh, Trey's muttered "oh my god."

Rane's blush deepens. "Well, yeah, but I wanted to—I guess—take you out to dinner."

"Why?"

"Well, you know..." He shifts his weight. "On a date."

*Date.*

That word I know.

The pressure of it hits me all at once. Rane, standing there in his nice shirt with his styled hair, asking me on a *date*. In front of everyone. While I'm lying on the floor in sweatpants with a textbook.

"Um." I scramble to my feet. "Yeah. Uh. Okay."

His whole face lights up. Relief and something warmer flooding his expression.

He's still smiling. Like I just gave him something he wasn't sure he'd get.

A date. I said yes to a date. My palms are sweating.

*Why do I want to impress him so badly?*

"Smooth," Kyron says behind me.

"Very romantic," Beckett adds. "Really swept her off her feet there."

"Shut up," Rane and I say at the same time.

More laughter. I look down at myself—old t-shirt, joggers, hair in a messy knot on top of my head.

"Um. Give me ten?"

"Sure." Rane's still smiling. "Take your time."

"White," Beckett says without looking up from his book. "Trust me."

I pause at the bottom of the stairs. "How do you—"

"Just trust me."

I bolt for the stairs.

Ten minutes. I can do this in ten minutes.

I dig through my closet until I find it—the white outfit. The one Zoe made me buy. Leather pants, lace and leather top, the silver chain choker.

I stare at it for a second.

*It's just dinner. It's just Rane.*

But it's not just anything. It's a date. A real one. And I want to look like someone who deserves to be taken on a date.

I put it on.

The leather slides on smooth. The lace settles against my skin. The chain is cool at my throat.

I grab the makeup bag—everything Mira suggested at the counter. I don't have time to overthink it. A single shimmer on my lids. Mascara. The lip gloss that smells faintly like vanilla.

I look in the mirror.

I don't look like someone who sleeps in alleys anymore.

I look like someone who belongs somewhere. I look like someone who could be wanted. Who could walk into a place and not get thrown out the back. I look... like I belong.

Deep breath.

I head back downstairs.

The living room goes quiet.

# Chapter 32
## RANE

The guys won't shut up.

"You sure you don't want to practice your bow again?"

"Maybe drop to one knee this time."

"'Would you do me the honor'—who even talks like that?"

"Shut up." I adjust my collar for the fifteenth time. "All of you."

Kyron's grinning from the couch. Locke's leaning against the wall with his arms crossed, but I can see the smirk he's trying to hide. Even Beckett looks amused, which is annoying because this was partially his idea.

Footsteps on the stairs.

I turn.

*Holy fuck.*

*I'm the luckiest man alive.*

She's wearing white. All white—leather pants that fit like they were made for her, a top that's half lace and half something that makes my brain short-circuit, a silver chain at her throat. Her hair is down, soft waves catching the light. And her face—

She did something. Makeup, that's it. Her eyes look bigger, her lips shiny and soft, and I can't stop staring. Her heels hit the last step and I forget how to breathe.

My heart does something I'm not prepared for. Not just want. Something deeper. Like recognition.

"Rane?"

I blink. My mouth is open. I should probably close it.

"Oh my god, Nova." My voice comes out rough. "You're stunning."

Her cheeks go pink. She doesn't believe me—I can see it in the way she ducks her head, the way her shoulders curve in slightly.

"You lucky son of a bitch." Kyron shakes his head. "Seriously."

"Hey—you got to make out with her." I shoot back. "Had her legs wrapped around you and everything."

Nova's turning redder by the second.

Locke pushes off the wall and crosses to her. He doesn't say anything at first—just looks at her, something soft and serious in his expression. Then he leans in and presses a kiss to her cheek.

"We're lucky men," he says quietly. Gives her a small smile.

Then he turns, grabs something off the table, and throws it at Kyron's head.

"Knock it off. Fucking neanderthals."

Vaelor catches the projectile before it hits anyone. "He's not wrong."

I step forward. Hold out my hand.

"Ready?"

She looks at my hand. Then at me. Then she smiles—small and uncertain and absolutely devastating.

She takes my hand.

We walk.

The restaurant is exactly how I remember it.

Tiny. Six tables crammed into what used to be someone's living room, mismatched chairs, candles stuck in old wine bottles. The kind of place you'd walk right past if you didn't know it was there.

My mom used to bring me here when I was a kid. Every birthday. Every time something good happened—or something bad, and she wanted to remind me that good things still existed.

Maria sees me the second we walk in.

"Rane!" She comes out from behind the counter, arms already open. "It's been too long. Too long!"

I let her hug me, kiss both my cheeks. "I know. I'm sorry."

"You're forgiven." She pulls back, eyes moving to Nova. "And who is this?"

"This is Nova." I can't keep the pride out of my voice. "Nova, this is Maria. She and her husband own this place."

Maria's face does something complicated—surprise, then understanding, then warmth.

"Nova." She takes both of Nova's hands in hers. "Welcome. Any friend of Rane's..." She glances at me, sees something in my expression, and her smile deepens. "Come. I have the perfect table."

She leads us to the corner—the quiet one, away from the kitchen, where my mom and I always sat.

Nova slides into her seat and looks around, taking it in. The cracked plaster, the old photographs on the walls, the handwritten menu on the chalkboard.

"This place is…"

"I know." I sit across from her. "It's not fancy."

"No, I—" She shakes her head. "I love it. It feels real."

Something loosens in my chest.

Maria's daughter appears—Lucia, maybe sixteen now, when did that happen—and takes our order. I get what I always get, spaghetti. Nova asks what's good and orders alfredo.

When Lucia leaves, it's just us.

Nova's fidgeting with her napkin. I want to reach across and still her hands, but I also don't want to spook her.

"So," I say instead. "Can I ask you something?"

"Sure."

"Did you ever come around here? While you were… avoiding the system?"

She shakes her head. "I tried to stay away from anything the Nightmare Order was part of. And that included the Academy."

"Makes sense."

"Besides." She shrugs, not quite meeting my eyes. "I knew I'd never be going to the Academy. So it didn't make sense to come near here. I just focused on not getting caught. Staying invisible."

The words land somewhere in my chest and stick there.

"How hard was it, Nova?"

"It wasn't. Not really."

I frown. "What do you mean?"

She shrugs again. "It's all I've ever known. My memories with my parents, before they died—they're not all there for some reason. And after, when I was on my own?" She picks at the edge of her napkin. "You get used to it, I guess."

"That's no way for a child to—"

"I know." Her voice is soft but steady. "But it's what was. So I learned. Made the most of it."

I nod. I don't want to push. Don't want this to become something heavy and sad when she's sitting across from me in white leather looking like a dream I didn't know I was allowed to have.

The food comes. Lucia sets down plates with practiced ease—her mother's recipes, the ones that haven't changed in twenty years.

I watch Nova take her first bite. Watch her eyes close for just a second.

"Good?"

"Really good."

I smile and pick up my fork.

But I'm not really thinking about the food. I'm looking at her—really looking. The way her face has filled out since she got here. The color in her cheeks. The brightness in her eyes that wasn't there those first few days.

She looks healthier. Stronger. More *here*.

"How are you feeling about everything?" I ask.

She laughs, a little exasperated. "Which thing in particular?"

"Fair point." I grin. "I don't know—what's bothering you the most?"

The smile fades. She pushes a piece of pasta around her plate.

"Well. It was Silas. But now..."

She trails off. Doesn't finish.

I put down my fork and reach across the table. Take her hand.

"Whatever it is," I say. "You can tell us... Tell me."

She shakes her head. "I can't. I really can't."

"Why?"

"Because he said if I did—" She stops herself. Presses her lips together.

And just like that, the warmth in my chest turns to ice.

*He said.*

Silas said something to her. Threatened her. And she's been carrying it alone because he made her think she had to.

I'm furious. Not at her—never at her—but at him. At the idea that he's trying to isolate her from us. Trying to make her think she can't trust the people who would burn the world down for her.

"Nova—"

"Can we talk about something else?" She pulls her hand back. Reaches for her water glass. "Please?"

I want to push. I want to demand she tell me everything so I can figure out how to fix it.

But this is a date. Our first date. And I don't want to ruin it by making her feel cornered.

"Sure." I pick up my fork again. "Tell me something good. Something you're looking forward to."

She blinks. Like the question surprised her.

"I don't know," she says slowly. "I've never really... thought about it like that."

"Like what?"

"Like there's a future to look forward to."

The words hit me somewhere deep.

"Nova..."

She looks down at her plate. I don't want her to spiral. Don't want this to become heavy when she's sitting across from me looking like *that*.

"Well," I say, leaning back in my chair. "I am very much looking forward to the looks on the guys' faces when we get home and you're still wearing that amazing outfit."

I grin. She tries to hide a smile but doesn't quite manage it.

"Did you pick it out?"

She shakes her head. "Zoe did."

"How does it make you feel?"

She thinks for a second. Then the smile breaks through, real this time.

"Kinda like a badass."

We both laugh.

She reaches across the table, straightens the fold of my sleeve. She doesn't say anything. Doesn't need to.

We eat. We talk about smaller things—classes, the guys, Zoe's latest unsolicited advice. Nova laughs at my terrible jokes. I steal a bite off her plate and she pretends to be mad about it.

It's good. It's easy.

But underneath, I can't stop thinking about what she almost said.

*Because he said if I did—*

What? What did he threaten her with? What's he holding over her head?

Dessert comes. Something chocolate that Maria insisted on, on the house. Nova eats half of it and then pushes the rest toward me with a shy smile.

"I'm glad you asked me," she says quietly. "To come here. I'm glad I said yes."

"Me too."

I pay the bill. Maria hugs us both goodbye, makes me promise not to wait so long next time.

We walk back in the dark. Side by side, close enough that our shoulders brush.

I should let it go. I should leave it for tomorrow, let the guys help me figure out how to approach it.

But I can't.

"Nova."

She glances at me.

"Please." I stop walking. Turn to face her. "Whatever Silas said to you—I need to know. We all do."

She's quiet for a long moment. I can see her wrestling with it—the fear, the instinct to protect us, the exhaustion of carrying it alone.

"He said they're coming for me," she says finally. Her voice is barely a whisper. "And if I tell any of you... they'll stop pretending you're innocent."

The world tilts.

"What?"

"He said—" Her voice breaks. "He said they'll come for you too. All of you. If I say anything."

I'm going to kill him.

I'm going to find Silas and I'm going to wrap my hands around his throat and I'm going to—

"Rane."

Nova's looking at me. Eyes wide. Scared.

Not of Silas. Of me. Of what I might do.

I take a breath. Force my hands to unclench.

"Okay." My voice is steadier than I feel. "Okay. Thank you for telling me."

"You can't—"

"I won't do anything stupid." I reach for her hand. She lets me take it. "But I'm not going to pretend I didn't hear it. And I'm not going to let you carry this alone."

She doesn't say anything. Just squeezes my hand.

We walk the rest of the way in silence.

But my mind is racing. Planning. Figuring out how to tell the others without making her feel like she betrayed a secret.

She trusts us. She trusted *me*.

I'm not going to let that be a mistake.

He threatened her. He threatened all of us.

And he thinks we're going to stay quiet?

He has no idea who he's dealing with.

She trusted me. That means something.

So when they come, we'll be ready.

Because no one touches what's ours.

# Chapter 33
## NOVA

The house comes into view and I'm not ready for the night to end.

Rane slows as we reach the front steps. Stops at the bottom. He turns to face me with something almost shy in his expression, which is ridiculous because this is *Rane*—he's never shy about anything.

"So," he says. "If this were a normal date—"

"Was it not?"

"If this were a normal date where I picked you up at your place and took you out..." He gestures at the door behind him. "This would be the part where I drop you off. Walk you to your door. Linger awkwardly on the porch."

I bite my lip to keep from smiling. "Awkwardly?"

"Very awkwardly." He takes a step closer. "And this would be the part where I try to figure out if I can kiss you."

"Try to figure out?"

"Overthink it. Definitely. Wonder if it's too soon. Wonder if you want me to." He swallows. His eyes drop to my mouth for half a second. "Wonder if I should just go for it or ask first or—"

I kiss him.

Not soft. Not tentative. Not the way Trey kissed me—careful and asking. Not the way Kyron kissed me—deliberate and claiming.

This is me. Deciding. Taking.

His hands find my waist and pull me closer and I go, pressing into him, feeling the sharp inhale he takes against my mouth. He tastes like chocolate from dessert and something warmer underneath, and when I slide my fingers into his hair he makes a sound that shoots straight through me.

I don't stop.

I kiss him like I've been thinking about it all night. Like I've been thinking about it longer than that. Like fifteen years of not being touched has built up into something that needs *out*, and he's here, and he's warm, and he wants me, and I—

I *want him*.

His hands tighten on my waist. He angles his head and deepens the kiss and I let him, let myself get lost in it, in the slide of his mouth and the press of his body and the way my blood is singing under my skin.

Time stops meaning anything.

And then the door opens.

"I told you to have her home by ten."

We break apart. Rane's breathing hard. So am I.

Vaelor is standing in the doorway, arms crossed, but he's fighting a smile.

"Shut up," Rane manages.

"It's almost midnight."

"*Shut up.*"

Vaelor's grin breaks through. He shakes his head, steps aside to let Rane pass. Rane gives me one last look—heated, promising—and disappears inside.

Which leaves me on the porch with Vaelor.

He's backlit by the warm light from the house, golden hair loose around his shoulders, looking down at me with an expression I can't quite read. Soft and somehow heated at the same time.

"Happy looks good on you," he says.

The words make me feel something I didn't realize I was ready for.

I don't think about it. I just move—up on my toes, one hand bracing against his chest for balance because he's so damn *tall*, and I press a kiss to his cheek.

He goes still. Completely still. I feel his breath catch under my palm.

Then I drop back to my heels and slip past him into the house before I can see his face.

The living room is full. Because of course they all waited up.

They're scattered around the room, trying very hard to look casual.

None of them are pulling it off.

"So," Kyron says. "How was it?"

"Amazing." I'm still a little breathless. Still a little flushed. "That food was…" I shake my head. "Yeah."

Rane appears from the kitchen, glass of water in hand. "That place is the best." He's grinning. Can't seem to stop.

"The company was better," I say.

It comes out before I can stop it. My face goes warm but I hold his gaze, watching his expression shift from surprise to something softer. Something that makes my pulse kick.

"I'm going to bed before you guys ruin this." I'm already moving toward the stairs, but I'm smiling. "Goodnight."

A chorus of goodnights follows me up.

I close my bedroom door and lean against it, pressing my palms to my cheeks. They're burning. My whole body is burning—not unpleasantly. Like something's been turned on inside me and I don't know how to switch it off.

I get ready for bed on autopilot. Change into soft clothes. Brush my teeth.

When I look up from the sink, the mirror is fogged.

I frown. Wipe at it with my hand. The condensation clears for a second, then starts creeping back from the edges.

The water's not even hot. I didn't take a shower.

I press my palm flat against the glass. It's warm. Not from steam—from *me*. My handprint stays clear for a moment, then fades as more fog creeps in.

I pull my hand back. Stare at it.

*What the actual...*

My skin looks normal. But there's sweat at my hairline, and when I push my hair back it sticks to my neck. The buzzing that started during that kiss hasn't stopped. If anything, it's louder.

I splash cold water on my face. Force myself to breathe. Eventually the fog clears and I look almost normal in the mirror—flushed, bright-eyed, but normal.

It's nothing. Adrenaline. The date. The kiss. Everything.

I crawl under the covers.

The buzzing doesn't stop. But it's not unpleasant. It feels like anticipation. Like my body knows something my brain doesn't.

*Tell me something good. Something you're looking forward to.*

I stare at the ceiling and think about Rane's question. About how I didn't have an answer.

I do now.

I'm looking forward to tomorrow. To breakfast with them. To walking to class surrounded by people who want me there. To whatever comes next.

For the first time in fifteen years, I'm looking forward to something.

I close my eyes.

The heat pulses once under my skin—warm, steady, almost like a heartbeat.

I don't fight it.

I fall asleep smiling.

# Chapter 34
## BECKETT

"I'm going to bed before you guys ruin this." She's already moving toward the stairs, smiling. "Goodnight."

We all call it back—goodnight, sleep well, the usual chorus—and I watch her go. The way she moves is different tonight. Lighter. Like something that was wound tight has finally started to unspool.

Her footsteps creak up the stairs. Down the hallway. Her bedroom door clicks shut.

Then Rane turns around and his face is wrong.

"We need to talk."

The grin from dinner is gone. Whatever was there when he walked in—the flushed cheeks, the stupid smile he couldn't hide—it's been replaced by something harder. Something that makes my spine straighten.

"What happened?" Locke's already pushing off the wall.

"Not here." Rane glances at the ceiling. "Kitchen."

We move without discussion. Kyron sets his phone down. Vaelor closes the front door properly, turning the lock. Trey's on his feet before I am.

The kitchen is far enough that she won't hear us if we keep our voices down. Rane leans against the counter, arms crossed, and doesn't look at any of us for a long moment.

"She told me what Silas said to her."

The room goes still.

"When?" Kyron's voice is sharp.

"At the dining hall. When he cornered her." Rane's jaw tightens. "She's been carrying it alone because he told her if she said anything—"

He stops. Breathes.

"If she said anything, they'd stop pretending we're innocent."

Silence.

I wait for Locke to explode. For Kyron to start strategizing. For someone to say something, do something, break the tension that's building in my chest like a fist.

No one does.

"They're coming for her," Rane continues. "That's what he said. They're coming for her, and if she tells us, they come for us too."

"So he isolated her." Vaelor's voice is low. Controlled. "Made her think protecting us meant staying quiet."

"Yeah."

"And she believed him."

"She didn't know what else to do." Rane scrubs a hand over his face. "She's been alone her whole life. Of course she believed him. Of course she thought the only way to keep us safe was to carry it herself."

My hands are shaking.

I notice it distantly—the fine tremor in my fingers, the way my pulse is pounding in my temples. I'm always steady. That's my thing. I watch, I wait, I anchor. I don't shake.

I'm shaking now.

"He threatened her." My voice doesn't sound like mine. "He looked at her and told her we'd be taken if she talked."

"Beckett—" Vaelor starts.

"He put that on her." I'm getting louder. I can hear it and I can't stop. "She's been walking around for days thinking she has to protect us. Thinking if she says the wrong thing, we disappear. And he just—he fucking—"

"Beck." Locke's hand lands on my shoulder. Heavy. Grounding.

I stop talking. My chest is heaving.

Everyone's looking at me. No one speaks. The kitchen feels too small.

I never lose it. I never raise my voice. I'm the one who talks everyone else down, who keeps the temperature low, who notices when someone needs space before they know it themselves.

I'm the one who watches.

And right now I want to find Silas and break every bone in his hands.

"This is what he wants." Kyron's voice cuts through. He's calmer than I expect. "He wants us angry. He wants us to do something stupid so they have an excuse."

"So what, we do nothing?" The words scrape out of me.

"We do nothing visible." Kyron meets my eyes. "But we don't leave her alone. Not for a second. Not in class, not on campus, not anywhere they can get to her without going through us first."

Trey shifts against the counter. "This is my fault." His voice is rough. "I should have seen what he was sooner. I was right there and I didn't—"

"You're here now." Vaelor cuts him off. Not harsh. Just fact.

Trey's jaw tightens, but he nods.

"That's not enough," I say.

"It's a start." Kyron doesn't flinch.

Locke's hand tightens on my shoulder. "He's right. We can't give them a reason. Not yet."

*Not yet.*

I hold onto those words. Let them settle into my chest where the rage is still burning.

Not yet doesn't mean never. It means wait. It means be smart. It means when the time comes, we'll be ready.

I take a breath. Then another.

"Fine." My voice is steadier now. Mostly. "But if he touches her again—"

"He won't." Locke's voice is flat. Final. "Because he'll have to go through all of us first."

No one argues.

We stand there in the kitchen, six men who've been waiting two years for something that finally showed up.

I'd never say it out loud. None of us would. But we'd burn it all down for her. Every last piece of it.

Something creaks overhead. A faint sound—could be the house settling, or her shifting in bed.

No one moves. It doesn't come again.

Silas thinks he can threaten her. Thinks he can use us as leverage. Thinks she's alone.

He's wrong.

And when he figures that out, it's going to be too late.

# Chapter 35
## Vaelor

The pan clatters against the stovetop louder than I meant it to.

"If you wake her up, I'm blaming you," Beckett mutters from the doorway.

"Pretty sure she sleeps like the dead." I pull open the fridge, scanning the shelves. Cheese. Bread. Some leftover chicken from yesterday. "Besides, no one's sleeping tonight anyway."

He doesn't argue. None of them would.

The kitchen has that strange energy of too many people awake when they shouldn't be. Rane's sitting at the table, turning an empty glass between his hands. Locke hasn't moved from his spot near the back door, arms crossed, watching nothing. Kyron's pacing the length of the counter—three steps, turn, three steps, turn—which he never does. Trey's leaning against the wall, jaw tight, still carrying the guilt he won't let anyone talk him out of.

So I do what I always do. I feed them.

The butter is on the counter over by the living room doorway. I cross to grab it, already thinking about whether we have enough bread for everyone, when I smell it.

Faint. Acrid. Wrong.

I stop moving.

"Do you guys smell smoke?"

Rane snorts without looking up. "Did you burn something again?"

"No." I set down the butter. Sniff again. Stronger now. Not kitchen smoke, not burnt food. Something chemical. Something wrong. "Seriously. Something's burning."

Trey pushes off the wall, crosses to stand beside me. His nostrils flare.

"Fuck." The color drains from his face. "That's not the stove."

We look at each other for half a second.

Then I'm running.

The stairs vanish under my feet two at a time. The smell thickens with every step, coating my throat, stinging my eyes. By the time I hit the hallway, I can see it—smoke, gray and curling, seeping out from under Nova's door.

"Nova!" I'm shouting before I reach it. No response. "Nova!"

The door handle. I yank my shirt over my head, wrap it around my hand. The metal is hot even through the fabric—too hot. I twist, shove, and the door flies open.

The room is on fire.

Flames climbing the curtains, eating the fabric in bright orange tongues. The rug smoldering, edges curling black. Broken glass scattered across the floor near the window, something charred and still smoking in the center of the shards. And in the middle of it all—

Nova.

In bed. Eyes closed. Not moving.

The flames are three feet from her mattress and she hasn't moved.

*No no no no—*

Trey's behind me. I feel him surge forward and throw my arm out to stop him.

"I've got her." My voice doesn't sound like mine. "Stay here. I might need to hand her off."

He stops. His face is white, but he nods.

I go in.

The heat hits like a wall. It's like walking into an oven, like the air itself is trying to push me back. I can't breathe—smoke everywhere, filling my lungs, turning every inhale into shards of glass. I put the shirt up over my nose and mouth. It doesn't help much.

The flames are between me and the bed, licking at the floor, spreading faster than fire should spread, like something's feeding it. I can't think about that. I can't think about anything except getting to her.

I move around them. Over them. Through them when I have to.

My skin screams where the heat finds it. I don't care. I just need to reach her.

I reach the bed.

She hasn't moved.

I scoop her up and she's still too light. I can't tell if she's breathing. I can't think about that either. I need to get her out.

I turn back toward the door.

The flames are higher now, angrier. Trey's silhouette wavers through the haze, and behind him I can hear the others thundering up the stairs, shouting things I can't make out.

I move. One step. Another. The heat is unbearable, pressing in from all sides. Something crashes behind me—part of the ceiling, maybe, or the bookshelf giving way. I don't look back. I can't look back.

The doorway. Trey's hands reaching out.

I don't stop moving as I pass her to him. "Take her."

Like it's not the most important thing I've ever done.

His arms tighten around her instinctively. "Is she—"

"Get her downstairs."

I don't know if she's okay. I don't know anything. I turn back toward the room anyway.

Locke and Kyron push past me with extinguishers, disappearing into the smoke. Rane's right behind them with wet towels, a bucket, whatever he grabbed on the way up. They've got it. They'll handle it.

I make my way downstairs.

My legs don't want to work right. I'm coughing and I can't stop, my chest is full of smoke and feels like broken glass. One hand on the wall for balance. One foot in front of the other. That's all I have to do.

In the living room, Trey has her on the couch.

She's lying there, still and small, and for one terrible second I think the worst. But then I actually look at her.

She's untouched.

The fire was everywhere. The room was an inferno. And she's untouched. A little smoky. Some black smudged along her cheekbone, her fingers. The sleeves of her sleep shirt are singed at the edges, fabric curling brown.

But her skin beneath is smooth. Not red. Not blistered. Not even pink.

She was in the middle of that and she looks like she just took a nap in a dusty room.

"Nova." Trey's kneeling beside her, hands hovering like he's afraid to touch her. "Nova, wake up. Please."

Nothing.

"Nova." His voice cracks.

Her eyes flutter.

She blinks once, twice, and looks up at him with an expression of sleepy confusion, brow furrowing like she's trying to remember where she is.

"What's going on?" Her voice is rough, groggy. "Why are you—"

She trails off. Takes in Trey's ash-streaked face. Looks past him to me—shirtless, chest heaving, angry red marks climbing my forearms. The smell of smoke everywhere, thick enough to taste.

"Holy fuck." Beckett's laugh is high and relieved and not entirely sane. "Holy *fuck*."

"You—" Trey's staring at her. "Were you *sleeping*? That entire time?"

"Sleeping?" She pushes up on her elbows, still blinking. "What do you mean? I just closed my eyes for a second."

"Nova." I move closer, lower myself onto the couch beside her because I'm not sure my legs will hold me much longer. My voice comes out as a rasp. "Your room was on fire."

She freezes.

"What?"

"Fire." The word feels inadequate. Absurd. "Your room was on fire. I had to—the flames were everywhere, and you were just—"

I can't finish. The image is stuck in my head and I can't get it out. Her lying there motionless while the world burned around her.

She sits up fast, wide-eyed, suddenly fully awake, scanning the room.

"Fire? But I—" Her voice pitches up. "Where is everyone? Is everyone okay? Where's—"

"They're fine." Beckett appears with a glass of water and presses it into her shaking hands. "They're upstairs putting it out. Everyone's fine."

"But how did—I don't understand—I was just—"

Water sloshes over the rim of the glass. Her hands are trembling too hard to hold it steady. I take it from her, set it on the table, and she grabs my hand like it's a lifeline.

Her fingers are cold.

How are her fingers cold? She was in the middle of an inferno and her fingers are ice.

The smoke in her hair smells like wood and char, but it doesn't cling to her the way it should. The way it's clinging to me, to Trey, to everything else in this room.

"I don't understand," she whispers. Her grip tightens. "I don't understand what's happening to me."

Neither do I.

But I hold her hand, and I don't let go.

# Chapter 36
## Nova

They bring me to the kitchen like I'm made of glass.

I'm not complaining. The couch was fine, but sitting there with Vaelor hovering and Trey still coughing and Beckett watching me like I might spontaneously combust felt wrong. At least in the kitchen there's something to do—somewhere to look that isn't three faces trying not to show how scared they still are.

Vaelor's already at the stove. Of course he is. The man just ran into a burning room and he's making food like nothing happened, except now there's more of it. Eggs cracking, bread in the toaster, bacon starting to sizzle.

That's when I see his arms.

Angry red marks climbing from his wrists to his elbows, the skin tight and shiny in places. Burns. From the fire. From saving me.

My stomach drops.

"Vaelor—"

"Sit," he says without turning around. "I've got this."

"But your arms—"

"Are fine. Sit."

I sit. But I can't stop looking at the damage. At what he did for me.

Beckett pulls out a chair across from me. Trey drops into the one beside him, another cough rattling through his chest.

"How are you feeling?" Beckett asks.

"Fine. Really." I look at Trey as he coughs again. "The better question is how are you."

He waves me off. "I'll be alright. We got you out. That's what matters."

I don't think about it. I just scoot my chair closer and put my hand on his back, rubbing slow circles between his shoulder blades. He tenses for a second, surprised, then relaxes into it.

"You inhaled a lot of smoke," I say quietly.

"So did Vaelor."

"Vaelor's not the one who can't stop coughing."

A mug appears in front of me. I look up and Vaelor's standing there, steam curling from the cup. The burns on his forearm are inches from my face and I have to force myself not to reach for them.

"Coffee," he says. "Drink."

I take it, wrap my hands around the warmth. Bring it to my lips.

"Oh." I blink. Take another sip. "This is really good. What did you put in it?"

"Sugar."

"Just sugar?"

"Cream and sugar." He smiles. "I should have known."

Vaelor goes back to the stove. The bacon's done, the eggs are nearly there, and he's moving with that easy efficiency he always has—like feeding people is just what he does.

I get up before I think about it.

"Let me help."

He glances over his shoulder. "You don't have to."

"I know. I want to."

Something shifts in his expression. Softer. He nods toward the cabinet. "Plates are up there."

We work in silence, setting the table, laying out food. Our arms brush as we reach for the same serving spoon and warmth blooms under my skin—not from him, from somewhere inside me. A low hum behind my ribs that I don't have the energy to question.

I shake it off. Keep moving.

Footsteps on the stairs.

Heavy, tired. Then voices—Locke's low rumble, Kyron's clipped response, Rane saying something I can't make out.

They come into the kitchen looking exhausted, covered in soot and sweat. The fire must be out. Kyron's carrying something in his hands—dark, misshapen, still faintly smoking.

He sets it on the table with a thud.

"Found this by the window," he says. "Someone threw it through. There's glass everywhere up there."

I stare at it. Charred fabric. Melted plastic. Something that might have been food once, rotting underneath the burn. The smell hits me—smoke and something worse. Something rank.

"What is it?" Rane asks, leaning closer.

"Garbage," Beckett says, frowning. "Trash. Someone lit trash on fire and threw it through her window."

I'm still staring at it.

*Trash.*

The word echoes. Harrick's voice in my head, that morning on the path.

"Fifteen years on the street. Sleeping in trash. Eating out of the garbage."

"Nova?" Trey's voice, careful. "You okay?"

"That's what he said." My voice comes out quiet. Flat. "Harrick. That day on the path, before I left. He said I was sleeping in trash. Eating garbage." I swallow. "That's what they think I am."

Silence.

Then Locke's fist hits the table hard enough to rattle the plates.

"Those fucking—"

"They went from threats to action." Kyron's voice is tight. "Words to this."

"I can't believe they actually did it," Rane breathes.

"I can." Locke's jaw is granite.

I look down at my hands. They're shaking slightly. I'm still wearing the same sleep shirt—singed sleeves, smoke in my hair.

"How bad is my room?"

They exchange looks. And I know whatever they say next won't be good.

"Most of it's gone," Beckett says carefully. "Some things might be salvageable. We won't know until morning."

The white outfit. The leather and lace that made me feel like someone who belonged.

"I left the white outfit in the bathroom," I say. "Before bed. I didn't want to wrinkle it."

"Then it's probably fine," Vaelor says. "The bathroom wasn't touched."

Relief hits sharper than I expected. It's just clothes. Except it's not. It's the first thing I ever owned that made me feel beautiful.

"The green sweater?"

Kyron's expression softens. "We'll get you another one."

"You don't have to—"

"You'll have another one." He holds my gaze. "And this time you don't get to argue."

I manage a small smile.

"So how do we prove it was them?" Trey asks.

"We don't." Locke shakes his head. "Silas's father would bury any accusation before it got off the ground."

"But it means we're not safe here anymore," Beckett says quietly. "Not like we thought."

"So what do we do?"

The question hangs. Everyone exchanges those silent looks—the communication they've built over years that I'm only starting to read.

"Nova." Vaelor's voice is gentle. "Until we figure this out—you should sleep with one of us."

"Your room's kind of gone anyway," Rane adds.

"Not to mention you slept through a raging fire," Trey says.

Locke's head snaps toward him. "She what?"

"Slept through it. The whole thing." Trey shakes his head. "Flames three feet from her bed and she didn't move. Eyes fluttered open like she'd just taken a nap."

"No burns," Vaelor adds quietly. "No smoke damage. Nothing."

Kyron's frown deepens. "That's not possible."

"And yet." Beckett's voice is soft.

They're all looking at me now. I don't have answers for them.

"Sleeping beauty," Rane offers with a weak grin, trying to cut the tension.

"Ha ha."

But I'm not really annoyed. I'm too tired. Too wrung out from everything—the date, the kiss, the fire, the realization that someone wants me gone badly enough to burn me alive.

The night winds down slowly. Food gets eaten. Plates get cleared. Conversations trail off into yawns. One by one, they drift toward the stairs—Rane first, then Kyron, then the others.

Until it's just me and Vaelor.

He's at the sink, washing dishes like it's any other night. Water running, soap suds, the quiet clink of plates.

I get up. Cross the kitchen. Stand beside him.

"Thank you," I say quietly.

He doesn't look up. "For what?"

"For saving me. For running into a burning room. For—" My voice catches. "All of it."

Now he turns. Those hazel eyes, warm and steady.

"Anytime, Nova."

I take a breath.

"Can I stay with you tonight?"

The smile that spreads across his face is slow. Real. He dries his hands on the towel and pulls me into a hug, and I let him—let myself sink into his chest, feel his arms wrap around me, solid and warm and safe.

And then I'm crying.

I don't mean to. It just happens—the fear and the exhaustion and the relief all crashing together, leaking out in shaky breaths against his shirt. His arms tighten. He doesn't say anything. Just holds me while I fall apart.

"I'm sorry," I manage, pulling back. I swipe at my cheeks with my hand, tears smearing across my skin. "I don't know why I'm—"

"Don't apologize."

My hand finds his forearm without thinking. Right where the burns are worst. I just want to touch him, to make sure he's real, to—

He inhales sharply.

I yank my hand back. "Sorry, I didn't mean to hurt—"

But he's not looking at me. He's looking at his arm.

I follow his gaze.

The skin is still red. Still damaged. But less somehow. The angry shine has dulled. The edges look softer, like a burn that's been healing for days instead of hours.

Neither of us speaks.

Vaelor flexes his hand slowly. Opens and closes his fingers. His brow furrows.

"That's..." He doesn't finish.

I stare at my palm. It looks the same as always. But there's warmth fading from it—warmth that doesn't feel like mine.

"I don't—" I start.

"Not tonight." His voice is quiet. Steady. "We don't have to figure it out tonight."

I nod because I don't know what else to do.

He takes my hand—the same hand that just did something neither of us can explain—and leads me toward the stairs.

His room is warm and dark and smells like him. He gives me a shirt to sleep in, turns around while I change. When we climb into bed there's nothing but exhaustion and comfort and the solid weight of his arm across my waist.

I close my eyes.

I dream of fire. It doesn't burn.

# Chapter 37
## NOVA

The living room has become my classroom.

I'm on the floor with my back against the couch, textbooks spread around me like a fortress. Territorial law. House history. Mark theory—which is ironic, given that I still don't have one. The words blur together after the first hour, but I keep going because stopping means thinking, and thinking means remembering that someone tried to burn me alive three days ago.

Trey's on the couch behind me, close enough that his knee brushes my shoulder when he shifts. Rane's in the armchair pretending to read something on his phone. Beckett's by the window with an actual book, though I haven't seen him turn a page in twenty minutes.

The front door opens.

Kyron comes in looking like he's been chewing on something bitter. He drops onto the couch beside Trey, lets out a long breath, and stares at the ceiling.

"That bad?" Rane asks.

"I filed the report on Monday. Apparently administration had additional questions." He scrubs a hand over his face. "Took two hours."

"What kind of questions?" I close my textbook.

"What caused it. What was damaged. Whether we'd noticed anything suspicious beforehand." He shakes his head. "But the whole time she's just looking at me like we did it to ourselves."

The room goes quiet.

I look up. Rane's jaw is tight. Trey's gone still beside me. Beckett's watching me again—that steady gaze that sees too much.

"What did you tell her?" Locke's voice comes from the kitchen doorway. I didn't hear him come in.

"What we decided. Overloaded outlet. Room was damaged, part of the ceiling collapsed. We're still living here, just avoiding that area." Kyron exhales, jaw tight. "She was already writing her report before I even finished talking."

"Think they bought it?"

"Who knows." He sounds tired. "She wrote everything down. Said they'd be in touch if they needed anything else."

Vaelor appears behind Locke, dish towel over his shoulder. "Dinner's almost ready."

We migrate to the kitchen. It's become routine now—Vaelor cooks, someone sets the table, we eat together like a family that chose each other.

It feels almost normal now. I don't hate it.

I end up between Trey and Beckett, across from Kyron. The food is good—some kind of pasta with vegetables and chicken—and for a few minutes we just eat.

"I've been looking into some options," Kyron says eventually. "Places we could go if things get worse."

"Like what?" Rane asks around a mouthful of bread.

"There's a property not too far from here. Off the main grid, but close enough that we could still get to campus if we needed to." He spears a piece of chicken. "It's not ideal, but it's something."

"What about asking the school?" I hear myself say. "There are other cluster houses, right? Empty ones?"

Locke snorts. "They'd never give us another house. We're already flagged."

"We could tell them about Trey," Rane says. "Make it official. Say we need more space."

Trey shifts beside me. "Would that even work?"

"Probably not." Kyron shakes his head. "They already know something's happening with him—orientation made that clear. But asking them to acknowledge it means more scrutiny. More questions about why our cluster keeps expanding when it was supposed to finalize two years ago."

"Any attention we draw right now just makes things worse," Locke adds. "Better to have our own backup plan."

Under the table, Trey's hand finds my knee.

It's light at first. Almost casual—just his palm resting against my leg, warm through the fabric of my pants. A small point of contact that shouldn't mean anything.

My pulse picks up anyway.

I take another bite. Try to focus on the conversation—something about sleeping arrangements and who's taking which nights—but Trey's thumb is tracing a slow circle against my knee and my skin is starting to feel too tight.

It's just attraction. That's all. The same pull I've been feeling since I got here, the one I've been trying to ignore.

Except it's getting worse.

The heat starts low, spreading up from my chest into my throat. I reach for my water glass, drain half of it. The cold helps for about three seconds before the warmth rushes back, stronger than before.

Trey's hand stills on my knee. Shifts from casual to concerned.

"—and if the Order starts asking questions about the fire, we need to have our story straight," Kyron is saying. "Everyone says the same thing. Outlet overload. Nothing suspicious."

I nod along but I'm not really listening. My shirt is sticking to my back. There's sweat at my hairline and I don't know when that started. The chair feels wrong against my skin—too close, too much contact.

I pick up my fork. My hand trembles slightly.

I glance down at my wrist without meaning to. The skin flickers—gold, red, gone. Heat pulses once, sharp and sudden, right where everyone else's mark sits.

Then nothing.

I curl my fingers into a fist and don't look again.

"Nova?"

Beckett's voice. Quiet, but it cuts through the noise in my head.

I look up. He's watching me with that careful expression, the one that means he's already figured out something's wrong.

"You okay?"

"Yeah." I reach for my water again, drain the rest of it. "I think so."

"You don't look okay."

"I'm fine. Probably just tired."

Trey's hand tightens on my knee. Like he's trying to anchor me to something solid.

It doesn't help. If anything, the contact makes it worse. Heat pulses under my skin like a second heartbeat, too fast, too loud. I can hear my pulse pounding in my ears.

"Nova." Vaelor this time, leaning forward. "You're flushed."

"I'm fine, I just—"

A knock at the door.

Everyone freezes.

We don't get visitors. We especially don't get visitors at eight o'clock at night, three days after someone threw flaming trash through my window.

Locke pushes back from the table. "Stay here," he says to me, and the command in his voice leaves no room for argument.

He and Vaelor move toward the front door. I hear it open. Low voices—Locke's rumble, someone else's clipped professional tone. Words I can't quite make out.

Trey's hand is still on my knee. Beckett hasn't looked away from my face. Kyron and Rane are both watching the doorway, bodies tense.

Footsteps returning.

Locke appears first, jaw tight. Vaelor behind him, his expression carefully blank.

"That was someone from Nightmare Order Security," Locke says.

My stomach drops.

"They want to have a conversation. Tomorrow. Eight AM."

"A conversation," Kyron repeats flatly.

"That's what they said."

"And if we're not interested in having a conversation?"

Vaelor's mouth twists. "This would be a required conversation."

"Fantastic." Rane drops his fork onto his plate. "Love those."

I should say something. Ask questions. Figure out what this means, what they want, how we're going to handle it.

But I can't focus. The heat is still building, pressing against my skin from the inside, and my hands are shaking and I don't know how to make it stop.

"Nova." Trey's voice, close to my ear. "Hey. Look at me."

I turn my head. His gray eyes search my face, worried.

"We'll figure this out," he says. "Whatever they want, we'll handle it together."

I nod because that's what he needs. Because that's what they all need—to see me hold it together, be part of the team, not fall apart over a conversation.

"Do you think this is about the fire?" My voice comes out steadier than I feel.

Locke and Vaelor exchange a look.

"It's not just about the fire," Kyron says quietly.

The room settles into heavy silence.

Trey's hand is still on my knee. The others are still watching the door to the living room, like someone might knock again.

But all I can feel is the burn behind my ribs.

And the echo of that pulse in my wrist.

I don't look down. I don't want to know.

# Chapter 38
## KYRON

I'm losing my mind in the bathroom.

This is ridiculous. I've shared space with her for weeks now. Eaten meals across from her. Watched her fall asleep on the couch with her head on Rane's shoulder. Carried her through the front door while she kissed me like the world was ending.

But somehow, knowing she's in my bed right now—wearing my shirt, waiting for me—has turned me into a fifteen-year-old who's never been alone with a woman.

I grip the edge of the sink and stare at myself in the mirror.

*Get it together.*

It's just Nova.

*Yeah. Just the woman who completes the cluster. The one you've been waiting two years for.*

*Though admittedly longer.*

I close my eyes. Shake my head.

*I've been waiting for her forever.*

The thought settles into my chest like it's always been there. Like I've known it for years and only just found the words.

I take a breath. Steel myself.

When I open the bathroom door, she's exactly where I left her—curled on her side in my bed, silver-blonde hair spread across my pillow, wearing nothing but one of my t-shirts. It hits mid-thigh on her. She looks small in it. Small and soft and mine.

The room is warm. Too warm, actually—I can feel the heat radiating off her from here. She's been running hot for days, that flush in her cheeks that won't fade, the way she keeps reaching for cold water like it'll help.

It hasn't helped.

I slide into bed behind her, keeping a careful distance. Not touching. Trying to give her space even though it's the last thing I want.

She shifts almost immediately, pressing back into me, and I have to bite down on a groan. Her body fits against mine like she was made for this space—her back to my chest, her ass against my hips, her legs tangling with mine.

*Fuck.*

I remind myself that Locke told us. That this is all new for her. That the kiss on the porch was her first, and everything since then has been uncharted territory.

I settle for sliding my arm around her waist. That's safe.

Except I'm not wearing a shirt, and everywhere she touches me feels like electricity. Even through the fabric, I can feel the heat of her—too warm, almost feverish—and my body runs cold enough that the contrast makes every point of contact light up like a live wire.

She turns in my arms.

Now we're face to face, her pale eyes finding mine in the dark, and she shifts closer. Presses herself against my chest. Her hand comes up to rest over my heart and I stop breathing.

"Nova…"

"Yeah?"

I let out a little laugh. Can't help it. "You're not making this easy."

"I just—" She presses closer, her forehead against my collarbone. "This is the first time in days. Maybe weeks. That I don't feel like I'm burning from the inside out." She looks up at me. "It's when you touch me. It stops."

*Fuck.*

"Not sure you should say things like that to me."

Something shifts in her expression. I watch it happen—the moment she stops thinking about the burning and starts noticing something else. The way her body is pressed against mine. The way my hand is splayed across her lower back. The way my cock is hardening against her hip no matter how hard I try to control it.

She shifts closer.

And then she kisses me.

I forget myself for a full thirty seconds. My arms come around her, pulling her tight against me, and I'm deepening the kiss before I can think better of it. She tastes like toothpaste and something sweeter underneath, and she makes this soft sound against my mouth that goes straight to my cock.

My hand slides under her shirt, up her back, feeling the heat of her skin. I bring it around to her side, my thumb brushing the underside of her breast, and I go rigid.

*Stop. She's never done this. You're taking advantage.*

I start to pull my hand away.

She grabs my arm. Holds me in place.

"Kyron, don't stop." She pulls back just enough to meet my eyes. "I want this. I want you."

"Are you sure, Nova?" The words scrape out of me. "I know there's a lot going on, and you've been dealing with—"

She puts her finger to my lips.

"I've never been more sure of anything in my life, Kyron."

I look down at her. She looks up at me. And then I'm smiling—slow, real—and she's smiling back.

"Then let me make you feel good, Nova." My thumb brushes over her nipple. She gasps, her back arching into my hand, and I have to swallow hard before I can finish. "You deserve to feel good."

I kiss her again. Slower this time, but deeper. My hand continues its path, cupping her breast, and she lets out a breathy moan that she clearly didn't mean to make.

It lights me up from the inside.

I roll her nipple between my fingers and she arches into my touch again, gasping. I use the momentum to roll her onto her back, shifting partially on top of her, bracing myself on one arm so I don't crush her.

I kiss down her neck. She tilts her head back, giving me access, her fingers threading into my hair.

"Kyron..."

"I know."

I kiss down her chest, over the thin fabric of my shirt. My fingers splay across her stomach underneath, feeling the heat of her skin, the rapid rise and fall of her breathing.

"Can I?"

She nods.

I push up her shirt slowly, kissing my way back up as I expose her. When the fabric clears her breasts, she gasps—the cold air of the room hitting her heated skin.

I pause. Look at her. Really look.

"You're beautiful, Nova."

Her cheeks flush darker. She tries to look away but I catch her chin, bring her eyes back to mine.

"I mean it. You're the most beautiful thing I've ever seen."

Then I lower my head and take her nipple into my mouth.

She cries out—surprised, overwhelmed—and her hands fly to my hair, gripping hard. I lavish attention on one breast, then the other, until she's squirming beneath me, making sounds that are going to live in my head forever.

I start kissing lower.

Down her ribs. Across her stomach. I feel her tense when she realizes where I'm headed.

"You don't have to—"

I pause. My mouth is right there, hovering over the waistband of her underwear. Close enough that she can feel my breath through the thin cotton.

"Oh?" I look up at her. "I don't have to?"

She squirms. Her hips twitch toward me without her permission.

"You don't want me to?"

"I—" Her voice is strained. "I just meant—"

I press a single kiss to the inside of her thigh. Light. Barely there.

"Are you sure?"

Her whole body shudders. She's losing the battle—I can see it in the way her chest is heaving, the way her thighs are trembling, the way she keeps trying to form words and failing.

I breathe against her center, letting her feel the warmth through the fabric.

"Kyron—" She breaks. "I take it back."

"So you want me to?"

"Please."

I hook my fingers in her underwear and pull it down her legs. Toss it somewhere behind me. And then I settle between her thighs and look at her—flushed and desperate and so fucking beautiful it makes my chest ache.

"Hold on to something, Nova."

Then I lower my mouth to her.

The sound she makes is worth every second of restraint.

She's so responsive—every lick, every stroke of my tongue pulls another gasp or moan from her throat. Her fingers are in my hair, gripping hard enough to hurt, and I don't care. I'd let her pull it out by the roots if it meant she kept making those sounds.

I slide one finger inside her while my tongue works her clit, and she nearly comes off the bed.

"Oh god—Kyron—I can't—"

"You can." I curl my finger, finding the spot that makes her see stars. "Let go for me, Nova."

I add a second finger, stretching her gently, getting her ready for me while I keep working her with my mouth. She's so tight, so wet, so hot—the heat coming off her is intense, like her whole body is burning from the inside.

I notice the air getting thick. Warm. Humid.

Steam.

There's steam rising from her skin, curling into the cold air of my room, and I should probably be concerned but I can't find it in me to care. I already knew what she was. This just confirms it.

She's fire. And I'm the only thing that can cool her down.

"Kyron—don't stop—please don't stop—"

I suck her clit into my mouth and press hard against that spot inside her, and she shatters.

My name tears out of her throat as she comes—her back arching, her thighs clamping around my head, her whole body shaking with the force of it. I work her through it, gentling my touch as she comes down, pressing soft kisses to her inner thighs until she stops trembling.

When I look up, her eyes are dazed. Glassy. She looks wrecked in the best possible way.

"Holy shit," she breathes.

I laugh—can't help it—and crawl back up her body, pressing a kiss to her mouth. She can probably taste herself on me, but she doesn't seem to mind. She just pulls me closer, deepening the kiss.

"More," she whispers against my lips. "I want more."

"Are you sure?" I pull back to look at her. "We don't have to—"

"Kyron." She meets my eyes, and there's no hesitation there. No uncertainty. Just want. "I want you inside me. Please."

*Fuck.*

I reach over to my nightstand, grabbing a condom from the drawer. She watches me roll it on, her eyes wide, and I realize she's never seen—

*Easy. Go slow.*

I settle between her thighs, the head of my cock pressing against her entrance. She's so wet, so ready, but I hold myself still.

"It might hurt at first," I tell her. "Tell me if you need me to stop."

She nods, her hands coming up to grip my shoulders.

I push in slowly. Inch by inch. Watching her face for any sign of discomfort.

Her brow furrows. Her nails dig into my shoulders. But she doesn't tell me to stop—she pulls me closer, urging me deeper.

When I'm fully seated inside her, I go still. Let her adjust. She's so tight, so hot, it takes everything I have not to move.

"You okay?"

She nods. Breathes out slowly. "Yeah. Just... give me a second."

I hold myself still, pressing kisses to her forehead, her cheeks, the corner of her mouth. Waiting for her.

Then she shifts her hips. Just slightly. Testing.

"Okay," she whispers, and pulls me closer.

I pull back and thrust in slowly. She gasps, but it's not pain—I can tell the difference. I do it again, setting a gentle rhythm, letting her get used to the sensation.

"Kyron..." Her head tips back. "That feels..."

"Good?"

"So good."

I keep the pace slow. Steady. Watching her face, the way her expression shifts from uncertain to something else entirely. Her lips part. Her eyes flutter closed. Her fingers dig into my shoulders like she needs something to hold onto.

"More," she breathes.

I give her more. Deeper. A little faster. She moans, and the sound goes straight through me.

The steam is back. Rising from her skin in wisps, curling into the cold air. I notice it in the periphery—the way the room is getting humid, the way her body is heating up beneath me—but I can't focus on anything except the way she feels. Tight. Hot. Perfect.

I want to make this last. Want to stay inside her forever, feeling her come apart around me piece by piece.

She wraps her legs around my waist, pulling me deeper, and the angle changes in a way that makes us both groan. I drop my forehead to hers, breathing hard, trying to hold on.

"You feel incredible," I manage. "You have no idea."

She laughs—breathless, surprised—and then gasps when I roll my hips just right.

"Do that again."

I do. She moans my name and I have to grit my teeth to keep from losing it right there.

The steam is thickening now. Curling around us, warm and humid despite the natural cold of my room. I watch it dance in the low light and feel something primal settle in my chest.

*Mine. She's mine.*

I slide a hand between us, finding her clit, circling it with my thumb while I thrust into her. She cries out, her nails raking down my back, and I know she's close.

"That's it, Nova. Let me feel you."

"I'm—Kyron, I'm gonna—"

"I know." I thrust deeper, harder. "Come with me."

She shatters.

I feel it in the way she clenches around me, hear it in the broken sound of my name on her lips, see it in the flash of gold and red at her wrist—

*Her mark.*

I blink—and it's gone.

But something else isn't.

A pull deep in my chest. A thread going taut. A click I feel rather than hear. Something ancient and certain settling into place.

*Her.*

I feel her heartbeat sync with mine for one impossible second. Feel her in a way that has nothing to do with bodies.

*Bond.*

The word rises up from somewhere instinctive. Somewhere that doesn't need proof.

And then I'm falling too—burying myself deep, coming with a groan, her name on my lips, the bond echoing in every beat of my heart.

For a long moment, we just breathe. Tangled together, sweat-slicked and spent, the steam slowly dissipating around us.

I pull out gently, disposing of the condom before gathering her into my arms. She curls against my chest immediately, her body finally—*finally*—cool. The burning that's been plaguing her for weeks is gone. I can feel it in the way she relaxes, the way her breathing evens out, the way she melts into me like she's never been this comfortable in her life.

"That was…" She laughs—soft, surprised, a little giddy. "I didn't know it would be like that."

"It can be like that every time." I press a kiss to the top of her head. "If you let me."

She hums, already drifting. Her fingers trace lazy patterns on my chest, and I feel her smile against my skin.

"Deal."

Within minutes, she's asleep.

I hold her in the dark, watching the rise and fall of her breathing, feeling the steady beat of her heart against my side.

The steam is gone. The air is still. Her body is cool in my arms for the first time in weeks.

Something changed tonight. Something finished. Or started.

I brush a strand of hair from her face.

"I've been waiting for you forever, Nova." My voice is barely a whisper. "And I'm never letting you burn alone again."

She doesn't hear me.

That's okay.

She will.

# Chapter 39
## Nova

I don't remember the last time I woke up wanting to stay exactly where I am.

I'm warm, but it's not the burning kind. And it's definitely not the fever that's been crawling under my skin for weeks. Just… warm. Safe. Kyron's arm is still around my waist, his chest pressed against my back, and for a long moment I just lie there, letting myself feel it.

His lips brush my shoulder.

"Hey." His voice is rough with sleep. "We have to leave for the meeting in thirty."

I make a sound that's not quite a word.

He laughs softly against my skin. "I'm getting in the shower. You should start moving."

His arm slides away. The mattress shifts as he gets up. I hear his footsteps cross the room, the bathroom door close, the water turn on.

I don't move.

I just lie there, staring at the ceiling, feeling better than I've felt maybe in my entire life.

Last night.

*Last night.*

The way he kissed me—like he'd been holding back for weeks and finally let himself stop. The way his control cracked when I pulled him closer. The way he teased me before sliding my underwear down my legs, that smirk in his voice when he said *"Are you sure?"* like he already knew the answer.

The way it felt when he was inside me. The way he said my name.

And underneath all of it—this sense of *rightness*. Like I'd made the only decision that made sense. Like my body had known before my brain caught up.

I press my thighs together without meaning to. Heat pools low in my stomach—the good kind this time.

I didn't know it could feel like that. I didn't know *I* could feel like that.

I want to do it again.

The thought surfaces without permission and I feel my face flush. I want to do it again. Tonight. Tomorrow. Every night for the rest of my—

*The others.*

The thought cuts through the haze.

I slept with Kyron. In a house full of men who are all... what? Waiting? Watching? I kissed Locke on the porch. Trey in the living room. Kyron carried me through the door while I had my legs wrapped around him. And now I've—

*They're okay with it.*

The memory surfaces. All those conversations I half-heard, all those looks they exchanged when they thought I wasn't paying attention. The way Locke said *"You don't need permission to act on what you feel. Not with us."*

They know. They're okay with it.

I take a breath. Let it out slowly.

Okay. Okay. I can do this.

I'm about to push myself up when there's a knock at the door.

"Come in."

The door opens. Beckett.

"Hey." I smile without thinking.

"Hey." He steps inside, clothes folded in his arms, and then he stops.

His eyes move over me. Slow. Taking in the sheet pulled up to my chest, my bare shoulders, my hair a mess against Kyron's pillow. His gaze lingers just long enough that my skin prickles.

Something shifts in his expression. Mischief. Like he's just confirmed something he already suspected.

*Oh crap.*

I feel the heat climb up my neck.

"I can explain—"

He shakes his head, that almost-smile still playing at his mouth. "You don't need to explain anything." He crosses to the bed, sets the clothes on the edge. "You're glowing. It looks good on you."

My face goes hotter. I can't help the smile that tugs at my lips.

"Here." He nods at the pile. "It's the best I could find after what happened to your room, but we'll figure it out."

"Thanks, Beckett."

He nods, his eyes holding mine for just a second longer than necessary—something warm there that I feel more than see.

Then he's gone, closing the door softly behind him.

I sit there for a moment, sheet clutched to my chest, smile still on my face.

*Okay. I can do this.*

I get dressed quickly—soft gray joggers, a black t-shirt that's definitely not mine but fits well enough. I can hear the shower still running as I slip out of Kyron's room and head downstairs.

The kitchen is full.

Vaelor's at the stove. Rane's at the table with his phone. Locke's leaning against the counter with a mug of coffee.

Nobody's talking.

That's the first thing I notice. The kitchen is never this quiet. Someone's always bickering about something, or Rane's narrating whatever he's reading, or Vaelor's humming while he cooks.

Right now? Silence. Like they are trying very hard to act normal. And failing, miserably.

I stop in the doorway.

Rane looks up first. His mouth twitches.

Oh.

*Oh.*

They heard us.

"So," Rane says, way too casual. "Sleep well?"

My face goes hot. "Um. Yeah."

Locke takes a sip of coffee. Doesn't look at me.

"Loudly."

Vaelor chokes on something. Rane's grin cracks wide open. I want to sink through the floor.

"Oh my god."

"Thin walls," Rane offers helpfully.

"Very thin," Vaelor adds, not turning from the stove.

"I hate all of you."

"No you don't." Rane's enjoying this way too much.

The laughter settles. I cross to the table and drop into a chair, burying my face in my hands.

Locke's voice cuts through, softer now. "You look happy, Nova."

I peek through my fingers. He's watching me—something warm underneath the smirk.

"That's what matters."

Vaelor sets a plate in front of me. Eggs, toast, fruit. I look up at him and he's smiling—that warm, steady smile that makes me feel like everything's going to be okay.

"Eat," he says. "We leave in twenty."

Right. The meeting. The Nightmare Order conversation that's definitely not just about the fire.

I pick up my fork.

At least today can't get any worse.

# Chapter 40
## KYRON

I can't stop thinking about last night.

We're walking to the administrative building — all of us, moving together like we always do — and my brain is somewhere else entirely. Back in my room. Back in my bed. Back in the moment when everything went tight and bright and I felt something click into place.

Not just physical. Not just good.

*Real.*

A bond. An actual fucking bond. The kind that's supposed to be myth, exaggeration, some historical footnote.

I felt it. I felt *her*. Her heartbeat syncing with mine. A thread going taut between us that had nothing to do with bodies and everything to do with something older. Something the system says doesn't exist anymore.

Maybe never existed at all.

We're cutting through the east quad when Rane gestures toward the tree line.

"Getting warmer finally. We should hit the lake soon."

"There's a lake?" Nova glances in the direction he's pointing.

"Just past the north boundary. Technically off-campus, but nobody cares." Rane grins. "It's where everyone goes when training gets too intense. Or when Locke needs to cool off after punching someone."

"I've punched you exactly once."

"It was memorable."

Nova's quiet for a second. "I haven't been swimming since my parents."

"Well," Rane says finally, giving her a moment, "when this is over, we're fixing that."

She almost smiles.

I fall back a few steps, letting Locke and Rane pull ahead with Nova between them. Vaelor's beside me, steady as always.

"Hey. Quick question."

"Yeah?"

"Bonds." I keep my voice low. "The real ones. Not clusters — actual bonds. Soul connection, fated, whatever. Do you think they ever actually existed?"

Vaelor glances at me. His mouth curves.

"Bonds? Like the old stories?"

"Yeah."

His smile widens. "You getting all romantic on us now?"

"Oh, shut up."

"One night with her and suddenly you're asking about soul connections—"

"Vaelor."

He laughs, holding up a hand in surrender. "Okay, okay." The teasing fades but the warmth stays. "I mean... there are references in the archives. Old texts, records that existed before the system. But nothing verified. Most Memory scholars think it was just how people explained strong cluster attachments before we understood proximity science." He pauses. "Why?"

I can't exactly say *because I felt one lock into place last night while I was inside her.*

"Just wondering."

Vaelor studies me for a second. I can feel him trying to read what's underneath the question.

"You okay?"

"Fine."

I'm not fine. I'm carrying proof of something that supposedly doesn't exist anymore. Something I don't have words for. Something I don't understand.

And I can't tell anyone.

Not yet. Maybe not ever.

Nova laughs at something Rane says up ahead, and my chest tightens. She has no idea. She thinks last night was just... good sex. A right decision. Her body knowing before her brain caught up.

She doesn't know what actually happened.

Neither does anyone else.

I watch Locke's hand brush her back. Watch Rane lean in to say something that makes her smile. Watch the way they orbit her without thinking about it.

Will they feel it too? When it's their turn?

Or was it just me?

I don't know which answer scares me more.

I shake it off. Can't think about this now.

We're about to walk into a room full of people who are going to be watching every move we make.

I've never seen the building they take us to.

That's the first thing that feels wrong.

I've been on this campus for years. I know every administrative office, every training facility, every shortcut and back hallway. I've never been in this building before.

It's tucked behind the main offices — gray stone, narrow windows, no signage. The kind of place you'd walk past a hundred times without noticing. The kind of place that wants to be overlooked.

We don't overlook it today. We're escorted to it.

Four security officers met us at the edge of the quad. Four. For a "routine conversation." They flank us without a word, and now we're walking through corridors that smell like nothing — antiseptic and empty, scrubbed clean of anything human.

Locke's jaw is tight. I see him clocking the cameras, the locked doors, the lack of windows. Rane's gone quiet, which is worse than his nervous chatter. Vaelor's hand brushes Nova's back, steadying her, and Beckett is watching everything with that flat expression that means he's watching for anything that could mean something.

Nova's shoulders are creeping up toward her ears. She's scared but trying not to show it.

I want to reach for her. But I don't.

Not yet.

The security officers stop at a door. One of them opens it and gestures us inside.

The room is small. Clinical. A table in the center with chairs on both sides — one side clearly meant for us, the other for whoever's about to sit across from us and pretend this is a conversation instead of an interrogation.

"Sit," the officer says.

We sit. Nova ends up between me and Locke. Good. I need to be close to her.

The door closes behind us. We wait.

One minute. Two. The silence presses down.

Then the door opens again.

One man. Alone. He crosses to the opposite side of the table and sits down without greeting us, without introducing himself, without any of the procedural niceties that are supposed to make this feel normal.

He doesn't need to introduce himself.

I know who he is the second I see his face.

The same sharp jaw. The same cold eyes. The same way of looking at people like they're specimens instead of humans.

Silas's father.

Laith Crux.

He's older, obviously — gray at his temples, lines around his mouth — but the resemblance is unmistakable. This is where Silas learned to watch people like he's calculating their worth.

Laith's eyes move across us. Assessing. Dismissing Locke, Rane, Vaelor, Beckett, Trey.

Then they land on Nova.

And stay there.

"Thank you for coming," he says. His voice is smooth, almost pleasant. Definitely wrong. "I'm sure you're wondering why you're here."

No one answers. We're not stupid enough to fill his silences for him.

"There was an incident recently. A fire in your residence. We're simply following up."

"We already spoke with campus administration," Locke says. "Filed a report."

"Yes. I've read it." Laith doesn't look at Locke. He's still watching Nova. "Electrical malfunction. Faulty wiring. Very unfortunate."

The way he says it makes clear he doesn't believe a word.

"However." He folds his hands on the table. "Given the unique nature of your cluster, we felt a more thorough conversation was warranted."

*Unique nature.*

I feel Nova tense beside me.

"What do you mean, unique?" Rane asks.

Laith's smile doesn't reach his eyes. "Six members is unusual. Seven, now, with Mr. Dalton's recent... proximity patterns." His gaze flicks to Trey, then back to Nova. "And of course, there's the matter of Miss Wilder's status."

"My status," Nova repeats. Her voice is flat but I can hear the edge underneath.

"No mark. No House affiliation. Fifteen years outside the system." Laith tilts his head. "You must understand our interest. You're quite unprecedented."

He says it like a compliment. It's not.

"I'm not unprecedented," Nova says. "I'm just late."

"Are you?"

The question hangs there. I watch his eyes trace over her face, down to her wrists — bare, unmarked — and back up again.

Nova's getting warm.

I feel it before I see it. The temperature beside me climbing, heat radiating off her skin like she's running a fever. Her hands are clenched in her lap and there's the faintest sheen of sweat at her hairline.

Shit.

I shift in my chair, casual, and let my hand rest on her forearm. Just a light touch. Easy to miss if you're not looking for it.

The effect is immediate. I feel the heat leach into my palm — my body running cold enough to absorb it — and her shoulders drop a fraction of an inch. She doesn't look at me, but her breathing steadies.

Laith notices the touch. His eyes track to my hand on her arm, linger for a moment, then return to her face.

*Fuck.*

"I'd like to discuss your childhood," he says to Nova. "Before the system located you."

"There's not much to discuss."

"Humor me."

Nova's quiet for a moment. I keep my hand on her arm, thumb brushing her skin, keeping her temperature down.

"I survived," she says finally. "That's it. I moved around. I stayed invisible. I didn't die."

"For fifteen years."

"Yes."

"Alone."

"Yes."

"No assistance from anyone? No help from any House, any individual, any... organization?"

The question has teeth. I feel Nova's arm heat up under my palm again.

"No," she says. "Just me."

Laith studies her. The silence stretches.

"And your parents," he says. "They died when you were eleven, correct?"

Nova goes rigid.

"That's in whatever file you have," she says. Her voice has gone cold. "You already know the answer."

"I know what the records say. I'm asking what you remember."

"I don't remember much."

"Nothing at all?"

"I was eleven. It was traumatic. Things are fuzzy." Each word is clipped. Controlled. "Is there a point to this?"

Laith leans back in his chair. Still smiling that empty smile.

"Just trying to understand how a child survives alone for fifteen years without any intervention. Without any support system. Without—" his eyes drop to her wrists again, "—any mark at all."

"I was careful."

"You were remarkable."

Again, it sounds like praise. Again, it's not.

Nova's temperature is climbing despite my hand on her arm. I press harder, trying to draw more heat, and her jaw tightens.

"I think we're done," Locke says.

Laith doesn't look at him. "I'll decide when we're done."

"You said this was a conversation. Conversations are voluntary."

"Are they?" Laith's smile sharpens. "I don't recall saying it was voluntary."

The room goes cold. Not temperature — atmosphere.

Vaelor shifts in his seat. Rane's hand twitches toward his hair — stops himself. Beckett is watching Laith with an expression I've never seen on him before.

And Nova—

Nova is burning up.

I can feel it now, really feel it — heat pouring off her in waves, soaking into my hand, more than I can absorb. Sweat is beading at her temples. Her skin is flushed. If this goes on much longer, everyone in this room is going to notice something is very, very wrong.

"We need a break," I say.

Laith's eyes cut to me. "Excuse me?"

"A break. Five minutes. Unless you want her passing out in your interrogation room."

I don't bother pretending this isn't what it is.

His gaze drops to my hand on Nova's arm. To her flushed face. To the way she's breathing too fast.

Something flickers in his expression. Interest. The kind I don't like.

"Of course," he says smoothly. "Take all the time you need."

He stands. Buttons his jacket. Walks to the door.

Then he pauses, one hand on the frame, and looks back at Nova.

"We'll continue this soon, Miss Wilder. I have so many more questions."

The door closes behind him.

Nova lets out a breath like she's been holding it for the last ten minutes. Her whole body sags, and I pull her closer, both hands on her now, absorbing as much heat as I can.

"What the fuck was that?" Rane breathes.

"That was Silas's father," I say.

Everyone goes still.

"That—" Locke stops. Starts again. "That was—"

"Laith Crux. Nightmare Order. High-level. And very, very interested in Nova."

Nova shudders against me. For a second—just a second—the heat eases. Then I feel it start to climb again.

"He knew things," she whispers. "He knew about my parents. He was asking about them like—"

"Like he already had the answers," Beckett finishes quietly.

"This wasn't about the fire," Vaelor says. "This was never about the fire."

No. It wasn't.

It was about her. What she is. What she might become.

And now Laith Crux knows something is different about her. He saw me touching her. He saw her overheating. He saw the way we reacted when he pushed.

He doesn't know what he's looking at yet. But he's going to keep looking until he figures it out.

I hold Nova tighter and try not to think about what happens when he does.

# Chapter 41
## Nova

The second we're outside, the light hurts.

And then I double over.

"Nova—" Kyron's hands are on me immediately, one on my back, one gripping my arm. The cold of his touch cuts through the heat for half a second before it's swallowed up again.

"I'm fine," I gasp. "I'm fine, just—give me a minute."

I am *not* fine.

The heat that was building in that room hasn't stopped. It's getting worse. My skin feels too tight, like something underneath is trying to claw its way out. Every breath burns going down.

"Keep moving," Locke says, low and urgent. "We need distance."

They form up around me without discussion. Kyron on one side, Locke on the other, the rest falling in behind. We're walking fast—too fast for how my legs feel, like they're made of something that's melting from the inside.

The grass beneath my feet is turning brown. Dying. I watch it happen and can't make sense of it.

"Uh, guys?" Rane's voice behind me. "The ground is—"

"I see it," Kyron says tightly.

We're far enough from the building that my body stops pretending. My knees buckle and Kyron catches me before I hit the ground.

"Whoa—" His hands are on me immediately helping me stand, both of them now, pulling heat as fast as he can. But it's not enough. I can feel it building again already.

"Okay, seriously." Rane moves up beside us. "What the hell is going on with you two?"

He's not angry. Just confused. Trying to make sense of why Kyron hasn't stopped touching me since we left that room.

He starts to add something—probably something light, something Rane—and then he sees me shaking. His mouth closes.

"She's burning up," Kyron says. "I've been trying to cool her down but I can't pull the heat fast enough."

"Pull the heat?" Trey frowns. "What does that mean?"

"It means I run cold." Kyron's voice is tight. "Always have. When I touch her, it seems to absorb some of it. But this—" He shakes his head. "This is different. It's too much."

"Let me try." Vaelor reaches for my forehead—and yanks his hand back with a hiss. "Shit."

"What?" Locke's there instantly.

"She's—" Vaelor stares at his palm, then at me. "She's actually on fire. It's not a fever. *Fire.*"

"Not helping," I manage.

"No, I mean—" He looks at Kyron. "How are you even holding her?"

"Barely."

The air around us shimmers. I can see it now—heat waves rising off my skin like pavement in the summer. A leaf drifts down from a tree we pass and curls into ash before it touches my shoulder.

My knees buckle again.

Locke catches me before I hit the ground. The sound he makes—a sharp, pained hiss—tells me his hands are burning too. But he doesn't let go.

"We need to cool her down," Trey says. "Ice? Cold water? Something—"

"The lake." Beckett's voice cuts through. Calm. Certain. "It's close. North boundary."

"Will that even work?" Rane asks.

"Worth a shot," Kyron says. "It's the only shot we've got."

They start moving. I try to keep up but my legs aren't working right anymore. Every step is agony—fire racing up my calves, my thighs, pooling in my chest like molten metal.

"I can't—" I stumble again. "I can't walk."

Kyron scoops me up without hesitation. One arm under my knees, one behind my back, pulling me against his chest.

He grunts. I feel his arms trembling.

"Kyron—"

"I've got you."

"You're hurting—"

"I've got you."

But he's not fine. I can see it in the way his jaw is locked, the way the cords of his neck are standing out. I'm burning him. Every second he holds me, I'm burning him alive.

"Put me down," I whisper. "Please. I'm hurting you."

"Not happening."

"Kyron—"

"Nova." His voice cracks. "I'm not letting you go."

We're moving faster now. Running. The trees blur past and I can't focus on anything except the fire under my skin and the way it's eating me alive from the inside out.

"Kyron—" Vaelor's voice, somewhere to our left. "Your eyes."

"What about them?"

"They're glowing."

I force my head up. Force myself to look at him.

Blue. Bright, impossible blue—not his normal color but something else. Something that's lighting up from the inside, like ice catching sunlight.

"Almost there," Beckett calls. "Thirty more feet."

I smell it before I see it—water and earth and something green. Then the trees open up and there it is. The lake. Glass-still and dark, reflecting the gray sky above.

Locke breaks off, scanning the treeline, the shadows between the trees. Making sure we're alone. Protecting me even now.

Kyron doesn't slow down.

He runs straight into the water, still holding me, until it's up to his waist. The cold hits my legs and I gasp—relief and agony at once, the fire meeting something that might actually fight back.

"Don't let go," I manage. My fingers dig into his shirt. "Please. Don't let go."

His arms tighten around me. "I won't. I'm right here."

He starts to lower me into the water.

The second my body submerges, something goes wrong.

It boils.

Actually boils. Steam erupts around me, the water churning and hissing where it touches my skin. The relief I felt vanishes—replaced by something worse. Something building.

Kyron cries out. His arms jerk back—red and blistered where he was holding me. The water between us is bubbling, steaming, too hot for him to reach through.

"Kyron—"

"I'm okay." He's not okay. He's backing away from me, and I can see the pain on his face, and I did that. I hurt him.

"Get out," I gasp. "Get out of the water."

"Nova—"

"GET OUT."

He goes. Staggers back to the shore where the others are standing, frozen. And I'm alone.

The water is boiling around me and I'm screaming now—I can hear the sound tearing out of my throat but it doesn't feel like it's coming from me. The heat isn't stopping. It's building. Climbing. Racing toward something I can't see.

Pain surges in my wrist worse than anything else.

I lift my arm out of the water and there's light there. Gold and red, pulsing under my skin, forming shapes I don't recognize. A symbol. Something that's never been there before, flickering in and out like it can't decide if it's real.

"NOVA!"

Someone's shouting my name. All of them, maybe. I can't tell anymore. The world is narrowing down to just the fire and the water and the thing that's trying to tear its way out of my chest.

The light at my wrist pulses brighter. Faster.

I throw my head back and scream.

# Chapter 42
## Kyron

The water is boiling.

I can see it from here—steam rising in sheets, the surface churning around. My arms are screaming, the skin red and blistered where I held her, and I can't feel anything except the thread in my chest pulling so hard I think it might snap.

*Nova.*

She's fifty feet out. Might as well be fifty miles.

"I'm going in."

Locke's already moving, hitting the water before anyone can stop him. It hisses against his legs—I see him flinch, see the pain flash across his face—but he keeps going, wading deeper, reaching for her.

"Locke!" Vaelor's voice cracks. "LOCKE, STOP—"

The water hits his waist and he staggers. I watch his whole body seize, watch his hands go under the surface and come back up red. He's still trying to move forward. Still trying to reach her.

Trey gets there first.

He tackles Locke from behind, dragging him back toward shore while Locke fights him—actually fights him, throwing elbows, snarling something I can't make out over the hiss and crack of the lake tearing itself apart.

"LET ME GO—"

"You'll die!" Trey's got his arms locked around Locke's chest, hauling him backward through water that's leaving welts on both of them. "You'll fucking die and it won't help her—"

"I DON'T CARE—"

Vaelor wades in to help. Between the two of them they drag Locke onto the shore, and he's still fighting, still trying to get back to her, and I've never seen him like this. Never seen any of us like this.

Rane hasn't moved.

He's standing at the waterline, arms limp at his sides, staring at her. His face is completely blank. Like his brain checked out and left his body behind.

Beckett's beside me. His hands are shaking so hard he's shoved them under his arms, and he's making this sound—low, continuous, barely audible. Not words. Just sound.

I feel all of it. Their fear, their helplessness, the bond pulling at something bigger than just me and her. We're all connected to this. To her.

And we can't reach her.

*I can't reach her.*

The thread in my chest is on fire. Not the cold I've carried my whole life—actual fire, burning through me, and I know it's her. I know I'm feeling what she's feeling. The pain. The pressure. Something building toward a breaking point that's going to—

She screams.

Not like before. This one tears through the air, through my chest, through everything. I feel it in my teeth, in my bones, in the place where the bond lives.

Locke goes still in Vaelor's arms.

We all go still.

The water around her isn't just boiling anymore. It's evaporating. I watch the surface drop—six inches, a foot—steam exploding outward in a wall that blocks her from view.

"Nova—" Someone says her name. Might be me. Might be all of us.

The steam clears for half a second.

She's standing in water that barely reaches her knees now, head thrown back, arms spread wide, and she's *glowing*. Gold and red bleeding through her skin like she swallowed the sun.

The thread in my chest pulls once more—hard, final, certain.

Then she bursts into flames.

### **END OF BOOK ONE**

# Thank You

Dear Reader,

You made it. You survived the system, the tension, the cliffhanger (sorry, not sorry), and you're still here. That means everything to me.

Writing Destiny was a journey I didn't expect—Nova's story demanded to be told, and these characters refused to stay quiet until I got it right. Thank you for giving them a chance. Thank you for trusting me with your time.

This book is for everyone who's ever felt like they didn't belong. For the ones who've been told they're too much or not enough. For anyone who's ever had to build their own family from the ground up. You are seen. You matter. And you deserve people who would burn the world down for you.

If Destiny set something on fire inside you, I'd be so grateful if you left a review. It doesn't have to be long—just honest. Reviews are everything for indie authors, and yours could help another reader find their way to Nova and her guys.

This is only the beginning. The Nightmare Misfits have more story to tell, and I can't wait for you to see what comes next.

CEECEE CROW

Until then—stay a little feral.

CeeCee Crow

# About The Author

CeeCee Crow writes darkly addictive romance with possessive heroes, resilient heroines, and bonds that refuse to be denied. She believes in messy emotions, found family, and love that feels like fate—the kind that grabs you by the throat and doesn't let go.

A chronic overthinker with a caffeine dependency and an unhealthy attachment to morally gray characters (yes, it's on her license plate), CeeCee spends most of her time talking to people who live in her head and calling it "work." She believes every reader deserves a book that wrecks them in the best way.

She lives in Wisconsin with her kids, a deeply opinionated cat, and the firm belief that the villain was probably right.

CeeCeeCrow.com

# Other Books By CeeCee Crow

Nightmare Misfits Series

Destiny

Chosen

Order

www.ingramcontent.com/pod-product-compliance
Lightning Source LLC
LaVergne TN
LVHW040135080526
838202LV00042B/2916